Other Electricities

Other Electricities

stories
Ander Monson

Sarabande S Books

LOUISVILLE, KENTUCKY

Managing Editor
Sarabande Books, Inc.
2234 Dundee Road, Suite 200
Louisville, KY 40205

Library of Congress Cataloging-in-Publication Data

Monson, Ander, 1975–
    Other electricities : stories / by Ander Monson.—1st ed.
        p.   cm.
    ISBN 1-932511-15-6 (pbk. : alk. paper)
    1. Keweenaw Peninsula (Mich.)—Fiction. 2. Michigan—Social life and customs—Fiction. I.Title.
    PS3613.O538O87 2004
    813'.6—dc22   2004014389

13-digit ISBN: 978-1-932511-15-4

Cover art: *Jamestown, North Dakota, March 9, 1966* by Mr. Bill Koch, North Dakota State Highway Dept. Collection of Dr. Herbert Kroehl, NGDC.

Cover and text design by Charles Casey Martin

Manufactured in The United States of America
This book is printed on acid-free paper.

This project is supported in part by an award from the National Endowment for the Arts. Funding has also been provided by The Kentucky Arts Council, a state agency in the Education, Arts and Humanities Cabinet, with support from the National Endowment for the Arts. **NATIONAL ENDOWMENT FOR THE ARTS**

Sarabande Books is a nonprofit literary organization.

THIRD PRINTING

This book is for Judy, who appears sometimes in radio and light,
for Terry, Ben, and Paula,
and for Megan who is my absolute, my X

A Table of Contents Provided for Your Convenience

INCLUDING BRIEF KEYWORD INDEX AND IDENTIFICATION OF

SPEAKERS/MAIN CHARACTERS, AS APPROPRIATE

Acknowledgments

I would like to thank the editors of the following publications, in which these stories, often in slightly different form, originally appeared:

3rd Bed: "Subtraction Is the Only Worthwhile Operation"; "Dream
        Obits for My Mother"
Alaska Quarterly Review: "Stethoscope"
Bat City Review: "Get Started"; "The Sudden Possibility of Nakedness"
Born Magazine: "Stop Your Crying," as "Trace"
Boston Review: "Big 32"
Conduit: "A Helpful Guide ..." as "Cast List"
Faultline: "Isle Royale"
Flyway: "Piñata"
Fugue: "Other Electricities"
Hayden's Ferry Review: "Consideration of the Force Required to Break
        an Arm"; "I Am Getting Comfortable With
        My Grief"
Indiana Review: "Intermittence"; "The Organization and Formation of
        Blizzards as Seen by Satellites: A–Z"
Mississippi Review: "Forecast"
Mississippi Review Online: "Freda Thinks Spring"
New Orleans Review: "We Are Going to See the Oracle of Apollo in
        Tapiola, Michigan"
Passages North: "Death Messages: Instructions for the Officer"; "Flare Up"
Pleiades: "Instructions for Divers: On Retrieval"; "Constellations"
Post Road: "A Huge, Old Radio"
Quarterly West: "Bowling Balls Sent Down Through Windows From
        Overpasses That Stretch Like Spiderwebs Above"
The Southeast Review: "To Reduce Your Likelihood of Murder"
Willow Springs: "Residue"

CHARACTERS AND THEIR RELATIONSHIPS HEREIN

We, general, royal—disembodied voice of the town, the weather, the mine, the school; a sort of Greek Chorus

Yr protagonist, radio amateur, sometimes vandal, at times perhaps the author

Her mother also died in a winter car accident years before; seems like everybody did

His mother will soon die

Young Officer, who has to make the family notification after Liz goes through

Sal Luoma, Chemistry teacher of; has an estranged and possibly delinquent daughter

Lannie Shutter, Shop teacher of

Vice Principal of

Timothy, her younger, snowmobiling, somewhat neurotic brother; loves water; dreams of teeth; maybe ends the world

Harriet, her friend and maybe (?) lover, who drives the plow and picks up Yr Protagonist and his younger brother

Stephen, her distant dumbass cousin, will rob a bank

Uncle, died in a mine

Jelly, went to prom with Harriet; returning home for Carrie's funeral

Sandy, whom he hits on while flying; big liar

Liz, the Central X

Elsie Prisk, grandmother of

Nina Poirier, dead

Family, members of

Ben, cousin, only appears briefly

Psychologist, who gets drunk at a wedding & sings Tom Jones

The Oracle of Apollo in Tapiola, Michigan, visited by Yr Protagonist and Liz before, who sees it all

Grandfather, gone to emphysema

Grandmother, gone

Father, king of radio and not much else

Mother, up and gone, but still somehow speaking

Brother, armless; aphasiac

Friends of

Jesus, goes to prom with Liz, goes through the ice, somewhat minor character

Tony, gone downstate, tells the Goat Boy story, leaves Bone alone behind

Tony's mother, dead, too

Crisco Hartfield, drops a can down a stairwell, breaks a girl's arm

Carrie, his sister, murdered (by Rosie)

Bone, his friend, dropper of bowling balls off overpasses; best known in terms of Carrie

Rob, his brother

Freda, wife of Rob, briefly obsessed with Bone

His older brother, Bernard, through the ice on a snowmobile

Henry Lumbree, Bone's father, a meteorologist; shovels Elsie out

Christer, pyro, collector of pornography, jumps off the cliff in the snow

Jesus, whom he compares himself to in moments like this

Parents still intact at least

Pastor Sam, had a stroke, recovered

Diver, tags the snowmobile after Bernard goes through, is a Van Halen fan

A Helpful Guide to the Characters

AND THEIR RELATIONSHIP TO DANGER, AND AN EXPLANATION
OF SOME SYMBOLS COMMONLY FOUND HEREIN

BEN
cousin; trying to kick a meth habit; helps put out accidental fires; some goodness here

BONE
bound for Lacy; friend of CHRISTER; not all that he appears to be; ROB's brother

BROTHER
armless; a possible aphasiac; loves fire; how did he get this way? good companion

CHRISTER
his older brother BERNARD went through the ice on a snowmobile; demolished junked cars with his brother with a hammer; possibly an arsonist

CRISCO
something's wrong with his ear & sense of balance; a shoplifter like us all

DIVER
brings up snowmobilers' bodies from the world beneath the ice; always encased in cold

JAMES ELLROY
crime writer; his ruthlessness is to be admired

FATHER
has retreated to the radio; an important force; user of many dangerous tools; guardian of the world of men

FREDA
repeatedly pushed down by her brothers in gritty snow & made to bleed

GRANDFATHER
dead of emphysema; formerly hooked up to a huge, metallic breathing machine

GRANDMOTHER
dead

HARRIET
her cousin STEPHEN will be arrested for robbing a bank on a snowmobile

CARRIE HARTFIELD
CRISCO's sister; raped & killed; Jesus that was awful & I hate to even bring it up, but it won't stay down

xv

JELLY	drives a rusted-out Aerostar; driver's side mirror hangs by a black cord that looks like a vein; flies in for a funeral
JESSE	went to prom with LIZ (just friends); lost his index finger & thumb in a bomb-making accident due to accumulated static; goes through the ice after prom with LIZ
JOSH	jumps off a cliff into the cold water & the dark below, the snow circling around him & falling on his body; compares himself to Jesus; drives his dad's car without permission; might cease to exist at any moment; minor character who is barely worth consideration
LIZ / X	dead by way of drowning; love interest / conundrum; went to prom with JESSE (just as friends); a central loss; always to be solved for, known as X for cross for crucifix, as variable in algebra, as always marks the spot
MR. LECHMAN	recipient of airborne eggs
SAL LUOMA	possible shoplifter; owns a lot of cleaning products; keeper of some hurt; great Chemistry teacher whose students die on her
MR. MILLENBACH	owns guns; a taxidermist; closest neighbor
MOTHER	gone to Canada or cancer; writes often but unintelligibly; the voice of radio schematic; visitor of many shrines; occupies a massive gap; exerts force even in absentia
ORACLE OF APOLLO	has the answers; lives in a shack in run-down Tapiola, Michigan; inscrutable
PASTOR SAM	had a stroke; recovered
POLICE OFFICER	his brother rammed his head through the wall when he was young & made him cover it up with posters of cars; his mother will die soon; it's his job to bring news of LIZ's death to her family

ROB	went through his deck up to his groin; required stitches for any of the many injuries he's incurred through his life
LANNIE SHUTTER	Shop teacher; access to lathe, drill press, circular saw, etc.; has a drug-dealing son; does not have all his limbs
ROBERT STACK	hosted *Unsolved Mysteries*
STEPHEN	the dumbass robs the bank in winter; what, we ask, is in the cards for him?
TONY	disappeared downstate for school; tried to cross the International Bridge into Canada with a locked safe in the back of the car; tells the Goat Boy story; his mother's dead, but if we had to itemize every dead family member of every character, this list would be impenetrable and far too long
THE VICE PRINCIPAL	checks on the kid in the Emergency Room who lathed off his thumb
DWIGHT YOAKAM	country singer
YR PROTAGONIST	the central character

— ON THE SYMBOLOGY —

ARMS & ARMLESSNESS	emotional availability; control; dysfunction; confusion; all that is sad & stole, inexplicable, & all too true; maybe the central story
THE BARN	ruined by huge snowfall; collapsed; a wreck
THE BLOOD	central metaphor; seen *Fargo?* Think of it—so red—on snow
CANADA	an underworld; an other country; an answer

CRIME	a way to act; a paradigm; speaks to the need to find fault
ELECTRICITY	the importance of connection; what keeps us moving, moody
FIRE	renunciation of fault, of guilt, of order; still, there's beauty there
FLORIDA	escape; a dreaming out; a postcard in the mail
FORD FAIRMONT	a womb; a mode of transportation; shows up throughout
FORECAST	a mostly accurate prediction
THE FUTURE	is there one or not?
HEARSE	carries the dead across the Lake to Canada
HUMONGOUS FUNGUS	symbolic of all bigness & connections; proof (possibly) that there is a God & that that is good (I guess)
LAKE	black & frozen over; Superior, primarily; latent danger; all surface until you go through it
MICHIGAN	more specifically, Upper Michigan, the Keweenaw Peninsula, former home of massive copper & iron ore mines; setting; snowbound; now in some ways a place only for ghosts & tourists; this setting
MINES	fault & silt & possible collapse
MURDER	for the TV news; a huge hole; a dark spot on the wall; much is measured against this; drives us apart; brings us together again
ORDER, ALPHABETICAL	sharp tool; snow wall; a plot
PAULDING	site of incomprehensible light
PLOT	think more in terms of grave

PROM   social function, a goal of sorts, letdown for
                        some but not for all, where we all want to go;
                        we will not all make it there

PUBLICITY   necessity for some; more dear than grace

RADIO   means love & loss & pine-away & frequency

SNOW   what accrues, accretes; a central player; a kind
                        of prayer

STARS   keep things in perspective; suggestive of
                        patterns & figures in the sky

TELEPHONY   all that wire & crime & electric charge must mean
                        something; one way of getting out & of connection

TOOLS   always threatening; they hang on walls & point to
                        the ground

TORCH LAKE   the cancerous water—maybe resonant with other
                        sicknesses

WHAT   the big hole; the impossibility of matching cause
                        to action & effect with any sense at all

X, SOLVING FOR   ( )

Other Electricities

Death Messages: Instructions for the Officer

T he snow is on everybody tonight—on upturned faces, reflected back in the irises of children in the window; on the hot back of your wife's neck as you know she's shoveling the snow at home; on the men chopping wood for the stove, warming themselves (as the Finnish proverb goes) twice. You can hear the echoes of the axework just barely through the winter air so thick with flakes. You are bringing the bad news to the family whose daughter went through the ice. This always goes to the youngest, they told you, the ones who haven't got seniority or sense to avoid the dark work. And you're it, just out of the old high school that will be torn down in a year, so you read in the *Daily Mining Gazette*, the newspaper that rarely reports on the mines anymore except in retrospectives and to say that they're still closed and still there are no jobs and the hills surrounding the town are riddled with shafts like holes in the body.

You have no holes in the body from duty. No bullets taken. You've never even been cut.

A girl through the ice with a guy. Elizabeth and somebody. You never remember men's names. Prom night and you're holding a gun and you're working, you're walking up some other girl's steps to her parents—only a year beyond prom yourself, that night that had held so much before you got it and turned out as empty as a fist, that night which you regretted.

Your breath forms fountains in the air as it batters the snow. A couple lights on in the house that you had to walk up the snowed-in driveway to get to. You are halfway. The manual says to make lots of noise on your way to the door so that you are not a surprise, to leave the cruiser's lights on for authority, to make sure that the parents are properly seated. You do all of this tasting salt, hardly making out their backlit faces with the fire open behind them and the warm air coming out to your breath and melting the snow. Inside there are pictures of the girl and you try not to look and you know you must come straight to the point and give them the news that is bad that is the worst that is good only because it's something certain, but nothing good.

You write down instructions on how the parents can recover the body—she is being dragged up as you speak but it is certain that the body in the base of the lake is her. They don't even understand what you are saying. You are back out the door walking backward, back in the snow that's half-down on the ground, a down on your body, a fuzz in your voice and your breath leaping out of your mouth and it's like you are eight again, your brother ramming your head through the wall and your lack of understanding, and having to cover up the holes in the walls with glossy posters of cars that gleamed in the bedroom light. You are shaking, as if you were the one receiving the news. You sit down on the snow next to the sidewalk, and then you lie back in it.

When you get to your car, the streetlight is out. There are kids throwing rocks at one another, but you won't reprimand them or take them in. The water main might be leaking and the pipes are frozen all over town, you're sure. Drunks on their way home troll the roads like zombies. City Council election posters hawk their candidates. All the animals in the street are dead below the plows. Your mother will die soon, you just know it now, no more holding on in the home with the iron bars of the bed and all the static on the radio since she can't tune it in quite right. And you know you must go back to her with this knowledge wrapped like a gift—a syringe or a prayer in your hand, hot on the back of your neck burning red and wet from the snow.

Other
Electricities

My father had moved up in the attic with all the radios and the best connection to the main antenna. He had gotten a call sign and had begun to shape the air with his voice. You could listen to him in the night. It was good to see him controlling something. Good for him and good for us. The night was filled with him, though you had to tune in right to listen—had to find his frequency and call sign, or scan the air for the rhythms of his voice. The night was filled with him upstairs and my brother and I below. You had to have the right equipment. Amps and SWL receivers. Mobile or stationary antennas, encoders and decoders, coaxial goodness. Circuit boards traced to spec. A couple hundred feet of insulated wire, shortwave radios, the code books, FCC licensing manuals. A license to use the language.

On the radio, they speak in code. Words that are not words. Words that are words, but not the words you think they are. That displace language. Shift it back and forth like light across a room as the day changes. Charge up the air. Charge right through it. Make it opaque.

He stopped going to work. He told us he had enough money stashed to keep us up for a year. He kept provisions downstairs and would make excursions down once or twice a night for salty snacks. He was always up in the night. Radiating some signal of distress.

My relationship with him was off and on, binary, like square or sawtooth waves. Like a switch. He was all there or not at all. Days he slept and nights he didn't. When I asked, he told me there's better reception at night. More range. Something about clouds. Noninterference from the sun.

Noninterference from the kids.

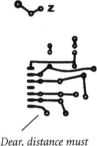

High cloud ceilings and reflection off the ionosphere (which is somehow denser at night) carry signals further. They increase your reach. I looked it up. I think he was saying something about grief, too. Some need to spread it out. Pass the news. That kid had died a week before. The latest in the string of deaths. It was like our father took it personally. It was like those kids—always someone else's— were in line for it. Like they had taken numbers and sat in the mall in queues. Getting drunk or getting dumb or getting ready.

Dear, distance must begin somewhere

You couldn't turn on the news without hearing about it. But the anchors related the news with no emotion, no surprise. Nothing to convey the importance of these deaths. You'd see their faces crease more when the DOW went down.

The Radio Amateur Is Patriotic. That's what the manual says. It is your responsibility as an amateur radio operator to pass the word in time of trouble, time of war. Time of danger or disaster. Time of tragic loss. During flood or blizzard. Pass it along. Make everyone aware. This is the Amateur's Code. You need to know it.

A guy held up the bank downtown in a snowstorm, took hostages, got taken out by sharpshooters through a huge pour of snow. It

Dear, distance = rate x time

caused quite a local splash—all over the papers, the broadcast news. Books being composed about it. Murder in the snow. The guy kept screaming things about being filled with voices. Conspiracies. The need for someone to listen. He found his audience.

He had a pirate radio station running somewhere in the area. You could hear him most nights on the low end of the FM, around 89.3 until the holdup, hostage-taking, and his death.

The Radio Amateur Is Well-Balanced.

I had got my own scanner and receiver and together with my brother I would listen for my father's voice on the radio in the night. We set it up outside in the shack with all the newspapers. We set it up above the words hidden in bags below the ground. Below the books that lined the floor. Below the gas line that we knew ran underneath. We hooked up the gasoline-powered generator to the radio when the batteries wore down.

The Radio Amateur Is Attentive.

We listened for my father. We always listen for my father. And we listened for who else was there. Another crackpot broadcasting in the night. There were lots of them, always someone crowing.

It is a life, the radio. Increasingly, our father's life. His father before him had the big old ones with barometers built in and vacuum tubes or huge coils. Installed on ferryboats moving across the Straits of Mackinac. Calling out in storms. Transmitting location, distance, weather, orientation. Useful news.

We knew he had a call sign. Everyone does. We searched the databases of current and expired and just-about-to-expire call signs for his name.

Nights would go like this: Have dinner. Wash the dishes. File away the food. Stoke the fire. Put your hands on the stove to see how hot it is. Don't burn yourself. Make sure the Saran-Wrap-like material over the windows is intact. Check for drafts. Watch your father go upstairs, say goodnight, get dressed, and go outside to reconnoiter.

—— *Dear, some forces act across any distance*

Our schedules changed to his. He wasn't available or as useful as he had been before. Got a cut or an abrasion? Knock on the door on the ceiling that holds the retractable stairs. If he's up, he'll answer. Bactine in the bathroom. Top shelf on the right in the closet. Directions on the box of Band-Aids: how to put them on; how not to touch the pad with your finger to avoid infection; how not to put bacitracin directly on the cut, but on the Band-Aid itself; how to keep the disinfectant uninfected.

If he wasn't up, we'd fend for ourselves. Which is not so bad. TV dinners for lunch. Sleep when we want. A lot of pop. Sugar cereal which we never had when Mom was around. We'd just go to the store and put it on our account. Bag it, bring it home.

He'd sit in the attic all night. He'd tell us sometimes who he'd talk to—some guy from Norway. What did you talk about, we'd ask, and he would not reply. Not really. Just shake his head and say something about transceivers or low-register noise, or bandwidth. Say something about something. We wouldn't say much in return. The Radio Amateur Is Nearly Always Loyal.

* ———— *Dear, distance is a section break*

One night while he was up top, we took the car. He didn't notice.

I drove it, gassed it up; we took it down to Paulding, Michigan, home of the Paulding Light. Which is not a light exactly. Nor anything exactly. It has no power source, no explanation, no obvious cause. It is not a hoax. It made *Unsolved Mysteries* one year. We watched it on tape a while after it aired, copied from someone who had recorded it from TV.

You go down this road and turn your lights out. You can only drive so far. Several miles down the path along the power lines into the distance— as far as an eye can follow—lights appear and seem to rock back and forth. My brother had never been there before. This was another electricity, I told him. Watch that thing.

The plaque said that it was the ghost of the miners who died in some accident. A likely lie. More likely some anomaly along the power lines— some collection of electrons. Some lovely gathering. Or power gnomes.

The lights move down the hill toward where you park. They come pretty close. Some of the kids who live around there told us the lights come right up to the cars and that you can see through them. Like electric disco balls spinning superfast, so fast they exert gravity or magnetism or some other force and cast off all the light that hits them. Tear the paint off a car. Tear your spare tire off the back. Tear hood ornaments right away. Even take a tie clip off a tie. A cross on a necklace off a neck. Here's the mark to prove it.

The Radio Amateur Is Truthful.

Dear, this distance is a light in Paulding

The regulars each had stories about the light. There was a group of guys who set off with walkie-talkies and a shortwave radio to hunt the thing down. If you hunt it, though—someone said—it won't come. This kind of mystery is like a source, a gas or kerosene lamp, a gas-powered or hand-crank electric generator. It gives birth to stories, powers them.

My brother was silent the whole time. Like he always is around strangers. And at night. Like he has been since whatever happened— without language, mostly. Armless, quiet. Sometimes words burst out of him, like Tourette's. Sometimes his voice comes in whines and shrieks. Sometimes he's lucid, conversational. I held onto his side for a while in the car, right below the shoulder stump. That's where he likes to be touched and reassured. He was wondering about Dad. I could tell by his expression, by his look of emptiness, by the way he held his cheek to the car glass.

I had a list printed out of dead call signs. We examined it.

N9AEP   TRACY A MONSON
WH2AEX   ERIC H MONSON
WD8AFZ   JOHN F SIMONSON
KB2ALI   JOHN R SIMONSON
KB5ASU   DAVID M SIMONSON
NV5B   ROGER N SIMONSON
WB5BBF   MARY G EDMONSON

KJ5BP   RONALD E EDMONSON
WD8BVO   ROBERT R SIMONSON
KA0BZV   DONALD L SIMONSON JR
K1CJ   ROBERT J EDMONSON
KB7CVT   LAURA L MONSON
KB7CVU   ROBIN L MONSON
N0DAPDE ETTE L MONSON
WB5DBF   THOMAS J EDMONSON
N2DEH   JOHN A MONSON
K9DGK   DARWIN T OSMONSON
N5DQM   PAUL S SIMONSON
N2EMV   MARVIN W SIMONSON
K7DRZ E   DON SIMMONSON

You couldn't tell much from the numbers or the names. We were solemn as if actually in a graveyard at night among the steam, stones, and plastic flowers.

I didn't know if you even had to have your real name to register a call sign. Or how you do it. Whom you register it with. The FCC? Some government commission? How much it costs. Whom to make the check out to. How long you get them for. Whether you can request a sign or do you have to take the one you're given. The Radio Amateur Is Curious About Things He Does Not Know.

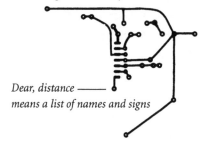

Dear, distance ——— means a list of names and signs

The Radio Amateur Is Cautious, Too.

The light didn't come up to us. It didn't tear the hubcaps off the car, or send us off wailing. We went home sort of awed and disappointed.

Dad was still up when we got back. You could tell by the light at the top of the house. Like the belltower in a church. Like Paul Revere. Like the strobe light up in the bridge to keep planes from ramming into it.

We had filled the gas back up to where it was. Exact. Reset the trip odometer at the right time so the miles line up right in case Dad wanted to take the car. Checked the oil like we had seen him do. I held the dipstick up to my brother's face. He smiled and it was fine. Black and thick.

On the kitchen table we found bits of further evidence. Printed out on a dot matrix printer—you could tell by the banding on the text. We didn't have a dot matrix printer, as far as I knew:

N0MWS 1999-04-02   FRED C. GEBHART, JR., TOPEKA, KS
N0NFM 1999-04-02   ELIZABETH A. LUNDSTEN, HASTINGS, MN
N0NFR 1999-04-02   PAUL A. TELEGA, DULUTH, MN
N0NFS 1999-04-02   DAVID T. GALE, SHOREWOOD, MN
N0NFV 1999-04-02   JEFFREY D. WILDE, SPRING LAKE PARK, MN

Look at that list. Like some litany of expirations. A register of those who voted for the wrong party. Landholders. A hit list. Amputation patients. Absentee parents. Those held in contempt of court. Those with past-date dues or bills that had gone unpaid for too long.

The Radio Amateur Is Knowledgeable.

Where does the power come in from? Generators, power plants, batteries. UPPCO: The Upper Peninsula Power Company. Through the lines we have been told not to touch. Through the lines we were instructed not to cut, even while wearing rubber gloves, even with large wire cutters with an insulated handle. The lines that come down in ice or heavy windstorms and twist across the road, stopping traffic in both directions. The lines that come alive. The lines that hiss and speak to my brother. The lines you can see reflected in his eyes. Lines that attract us like anything that can kill.

*

———— *My lead slug, my dial tone, my dumb luck, my instant, distant coffee, dear*

I know about the phones. While our dad was upstairs broadcasting something to the world, and we were listening in, or trying to find his frequency for his voice, his name, his call sign across our receiver, we would give up and go out in the snow around the neighborhood with a phone rigged with alligator clips so we could listen in on others' conversations.

There's something nearly sexual about this, hearing what other people are saying to their lovers, children, cousins, psychics, pastors, debtors. I would hold the phone for my brother while he listened. He'd whistle when something good was going on, or something nasty.

The Radio Amateur, However, Is Not A Voyeur, However It Might Seem.

All you have to do is find the junction box on the back of a house, or a larger junction box out by the road underneath the power lines (which we were never allowed to touch). Open it up and clip in to a tough discussion, to a life. You could make calls too, which we did sometimes. But not often because we could call from home. And who would we call? I talked to the FCC to find out who I'd have to talk to in order to get a ham radio call sign. They gave me another number. Everything is pinned to a number. Everything is handled by a tone.

Some stations just broadcast numbers. The key to some code. Something of national importance. They beam streams of digits into the night. No other programming. No anger. No malice. No bereavement. Curiosity. Politics. Love.

The Radio Amateur Is Sometimes Nosy.

We would take down messages and numbers. We would write down frequencies of tones we found on the Internet. We would go through trash out back of the Michigan Bell facility for manuals and pages of codes and notes. Diagrams. Schematics. We accumulated quite a stash of operating instructions for phone equipment. We stacked them in the shed with the rotting paper on the floor, with the words hidden below the floor in bags. We surrounded ourselves in them. They were warm when left alone, like compost. They were warm when touched or burned.

*

Yellow light from streetlights filters down through snow. Or snow filters down through streetlight light. It's hard to tell which. One is moving, one is still. My brother and I are using my pellet gun to shoot out light bulbs installed in motion detector lights on people's stairways. The Radio Amateur Is Adept With Guns.

It is good to walk through snow, to let it alight on your face as you turn up to the patterns in the sky. You can stretch out your tongue like a lizard and wait for flakes, but leaving your eyes open and allowing snow to melt on your cornea—getting bigger and bigger, you'd think, though snowflakes don't fall directly down; they shift from side to side and you can never just watch one come in; it's more like a frigid ambush when they get you—is what really marks you as being serious about sensation.

The Radio Amateur Values Sensation.

The Radio Amateur Is Friendly.

A plow comes slowly by with its lights whirling on top. We wave it down and she—an anomaly, a female driver—stops for us. The plowmen usually grin and let us in. They don't have so much to do. They make good money plowing the roads in the early morning, or whenever they are called to duty. But it is dull, I think. They are lonely mostly. They like company and conversation. Hot coffee, or too-sweet cappuccino that tastes like cocoa.

She's wearing latex gloves. She's listening to music—some old AC/DC: Who Made Who—on a boombox with a fading battery. It goes in and out while my armless brother holds it on his lap. She wants to know where we're from or where we're going. Which is nowhere. We are out walking. Our dad is upstairs in the house with the lights off surrounded by radio equipment. It's hard to come out with this, though. I point to my pellet gun. She nods as if she understands. My brother nods, too.

We are brothers. We are in tandem. We share secrets, cans of pop, the saliva collected in the bottoms of pop cans that makes up a small percentage of the fluid by volume as you reach the end. We share stories and last names.

You don't usually think a lot about those who plow the road. I mean, you think about the fact that the roads are plowed, and if they're not, you write letters of complaint to the city which are most likely ignored, because if the roads aren't plowed, there's usually a good reason—such as the finite (but large) budget for plowing having been plowed through already due to heavy early winter snow. You don't think about the drivers of the plows, their likes and dislikes, turn-ons and such, unless you ride along with them.

Unless you get into cars left unattended in darkness or daylight. You can find out a lot by getting into cars or abandoned machinery. People keep stuff under seats you wouldn't expect. Guns. Money. Building Plans. Pornography. Bibles and other books. *The Anarchist's Cookbook.* Cigarettes are a big one. Liquor in flasks. Half-frozen beers that explode when they open. Love notes and other things scrawled on napkins. Things that might cause grief if found.

The Longer The Radio Amateur Thinks About Things, The More Intricate They Become.

"It's not as interesting as it seems, kid," the plowman says, seeing my eyes jumping back and forth.

It has a lot of lighted dials and gauges that measure fluid levels or power. They flicker and dance when the plow jerks forward, their levels momentarily going down or up.

"I know. I've been in a few," I say.

She doesn't have much to say, which is unusual. You don't have to carry the conversation normally. You just sit alongside. Sit and listen. Listen to the on and off radio. Or the sound of the plow moving over concrete. Maybe a whump if it hits a dog or a drunk. You learn things about people.

She wears a business suit. I ask her about it. She says she's got a job interview in a couple hours and doesn't want to miss it, and what with the roads like this, she's better off taking the plow to the interview. I nod as if I understand.

She asks about my brother and I look to him. He doesn't answer, really. He hums low, trying to match the pitch of the machine. It's weird when he's really close to it because you can hear the sound beating back and forth as his pitch approaches the plow's. Then they're right in tune, and when the plowman shifts gears my brother has to play catch-up.

She gets us a mile and a half down the road before letting us out. I give her the Whatchamacallit bar I have in my pocket. The Radio Amateur, As You Know, Is Generous.

She grins and thanks me. Takes off her latex glove to grab it, shake my hand. Offers a hand to my brother, but then there's awkwardness as we pause and she retracts her hand. Her face is odd in the light that comes on when we open the door.

We get out and our breath looses itself into the air.

The plow moves down the road, burying a GMC pickup truck in a driveway.

I wonder about those latex gloves.

We make sounds with our throat, pretend we're dragons.

The Radio Amateur Is Meticulous About Appearing Hygienic.

It is later and I am telling my brother about how I only fake-wash my hands most of the time. Leave the water running long enough and divert its stream so if someone was listening, it would seem like you're doing it. Wet the soap on the top and the bottom so it looks like it's used. Always leave your hands wet in case someone checks them to see if they're washed. The Radio Amateur Is Cunning. The Radio Amateur Will Not Be Found Out.

The Radio Amateur Remembers When He Was Young, Right Before His Brother Was Born, How He'd Have To Be Driven Around In The Old Ford Fairmont Before He'd Sleep, And Even After That Car Was Long Dead And His Brother Was Alive And Without Arms, He'd Have To Rock Himself Side-to-Side To Conjure Sleep.

The Radio Amateur Remembers That Back-and-Forth. Like The Sea Or Static. That Lovely Oscillation. That Necessary Motion.

The Radio Amateur Wonders How Anything Holds Together.

We get back to the house and the lights are still off. We check some frequencies in the shed to see if Dad's still broadcasting. It's hard to figure out what they're saying out there. It's mostly mundane stuff peppered in with Bravos and Zebras and numbers tossed around like they must mean something. I think of things I'd like to tell him if only we had it set up to speak. But that equipment is much more expensive. Listening is cheap, nearly free.

There's a voice talking about the recent winter death. Probably he must be from around here. His name—he says it, unlike many—is Louie Kepler, from Lake Linden-Hubbell. It is such a tragedy. When will these kids ever learn. Was he drunk? I think he must have been. Doesn't it all come down to morals, family values? Doesn't it come down to parents ruling with an iron fist? Didn't the kid know not to go out on the ice? Didn't he see it coming?

The Radio Amateur Is Not Presumptuous.

Maybe he did see it coming, I say—though not on the air, since we don't have broadcasting equipment yet. Maybe he wanted it to come. Maybe he waited his whole life for something and it didn't come, so this was just as good to him. There are reasons to want to die. To want out of it. Maybe he felt some pressure. How do you know, I say, how do you know anything, you old ham fuck.

The Radio Amateur Is Empathetic.

The Radio Amateur Holds His Position If He's Sure It's Right.

The Radio Amateur Protects His Brother At All Costs.

I know nothing will bring the kid back, should he want to come back at all. I know I am not speaking to Mr. Kepler as if on the phone, nor listening to his private conversation. I doubt my words would have any more effect on him. But I think of putting a rock through his window, if only I learned where he lived.

It would be nice to be able to say it, to shove it in his face.

The Radio Amateur Knows That Power Used Is Power Lost.

The Radio Amateur Understands Needing To Know So Bad That You're Willing To Take It Home All The Way Through The Ice And See Where That Gets You.

The Radio Amateur Knows Enough To Not Reveal Or Hide Himself Away Too Long.

The Radio Amateur Is Not His Father.

The Radio Amateur Knows To Go To Bed When The Sun Comes Up.

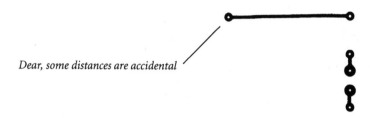

Dear, some distances are accidental

Intermittence

There is something coming through the trees and Harriet knows it as she closes the window on the winter cabin. The something coming through the trees is wild and white like a buzzbomb like a blizzard. The blizzard coming through the trees is more than snow multiplied by wind; it is more than wind divided by velocity over time; it is more than time resisting any change. Her library books are overdue, she thinks, as the remaining light seeps away and she is left in evening with the first burst of winter coming. She is alone and the roads away from the cabin will be filled and soon impassable with snow (except for plows—hers downtown in the lot). She has supplies—she always is prepared for the season's unexpected craft, but her books will accrue fines the longer she is away from the library, from the after-hours book drop, from the concrete-lined bank depository next door. If the winter lasts as long as it might, the interest and the fines could thicken into a wall of debt which she will not get out from like her parents and their periodic bankruptcies. If her parents couldn't stand up to the fire of finance and budget then maybe neither can she. If her uncle died in a sauna as the rocks grew slowly cold when the electricity went out, then maybe she will, too. If her uncle was a drunk who threw his empty liquor bottles into the canal with notes stashed inside—such a romantic sentiment for a sad man—then maybe she can survive what comes down to her in blood. If her uncle was the only family member who understood her wish to be an artist and he died anyway, maybe that wish is null and void, the product of wine and story, zero sum and dumb.

The snow comes through the trees in waves. It is not just snow but intermittent radio waves filtering through snow like water reverberating through charcoal crust in the sewage treatment plant, and moving back through the pipes to houses and the water towers that the civil engineers made of concrete and mathematics. The snow is radio, is water plus cold, is slow dance at prom and bad-haired-everyone circling each other, hands on hips and glossy necks, then going home to sex or loneliness or fire or guilt.

Harriet opens the door to go out in it, to bear its weight on her body. And it does have weight—incremental pressure distributed on the skin, that wide and tender organ. Incremental increases in her fines, even as she takes the crystallized snow in her mouth that goes to water on her tongue.

This snow is a marker of her guilt for letting Jelly down after prom. This snow is a marker that she is still behind. This snow is Liz, whom she knew so well from school, who came to that awful end so undeserved. This snow is the weight of water hanging in the air for miles above into the atmospheric curve. This snow is agriculture to this place—blood and body of the bird, the balsa tourist body, the bringers-in of money, the force that keeps skis and snowshoes up and moving, that keeps the Vacationland motel fat with snowmobilers, who come in toting liquor and littering their bottles in the rivers and the frozen roads. This snow holds the body of her drunk uncle now gone, is crystallized around his ashes that Harriet released into Lake Superior after his death—the lake that holds the remains of so many ships gone down on rocks, storm-prey; that holds so much iron ore and copper released back to the earth by ships' ruptured hulls; that holds the remains of men which are made of the remains of animals and vegetation; how great that eco-circle is. This snow is personal and comes down like it's meant to pierce Harriet's skin like Jarts, those heavy-headed lawn darts made illegal after the nth recreational death. This snow is displaced anger from Liz, and Crisco's sister Carrie, and Harriet's uncle who I will remind you died in the sauna that was not hot but had grown cold and his body had sat for days—this story is grotesque, a mask, but true. This snow holds the arrest of Harriet's distant cousin Stephen, odd guy and soon-to-be bank robber, who will rob a bank in February with a hundred inches of snow catastrophic on the ground. He will rob a bank with a twelve-gauge shotgun his father gave him for his tenth birthday, just before he died, which is sad I guess but never mind. Her cousin Stephen who—desperate for money, too, after the last mine in White Pine closes—will rob the bank with a shotgun pointed like a kiss at the white throat of the clerk, but no intent to harm. He will either A: take hostages in his sudden desperation, then be taken down by a professional SWAT team, his body in slow-motion on the television news, and even the hostages saddened by this outcome since he didn't seem so bad, they'll say; or B: escape on snowmobile because the cops will not be able to follow him as he flies alcoholic through the woods. Stephen who will rob a bank and leave a clear snow trail through the woods, who will rob a bank and be shot or caught, who will be shot or caught and sentenced, who will be *taken down* as the professionals tell it, or sentenced to years in jail where at least he will not be in need or out of work anymore, or drunk, where at least he will be fed and—sort of—loved.

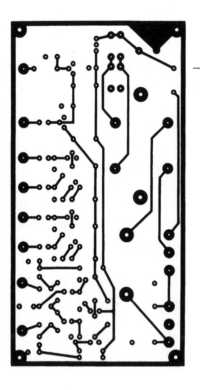

Dear, distance is a wire & solder story,
unstoppable like fire in high fire season

Stethoscope

There's something wrong with Crisco's ear. This is before the thing with his sister and her attacker, and this is before Liz goes through the ice in that old Toyota and leaves me here alone. Crisco's ear is whining, he complains, or is maybe whirring, or ringing. Regardless, he says (wearing a sweater that is more hole than fabric bought from St. Vincent de Paul), when it happens he can barely breathe. We tell him go to the doctor but he won't listen to us. He doesn't trust the doctors with their gleaming tools and stethoscopes and latex gloves all laid out on trays. I always steal a pocketful of latex gloves when I go in, or a tongue depressor. But Crisco's mother never trusted doctors either, on account of they took out a healthy kidney that they thought had gone bad. "It's just going to go away," is what he says as we stand outside The Doghouse skipping school, contemplating going in for a drink to use our fake IDs that are unconvincing but good enough we hope. We tell him—Jesse and I, Jesse whose appetite is legend, who went through a rotten bit of his deck all the way up to the groin, who will later go to prom with Liz (just as friends) and to their shared & awful end. We tell him everything we know about health, most of which we learned in class, sad to say. Crisco gets dizzy and I think it has something to do with the cochlea or with his family life or with the future and its plans for him—a premonition or glance, a preview, trailer, some ink print or bone sense of coming weather. It is day and the second largest suspension bridge in North America is up, holding back traffic while the *Ranger III* passes underneath on the way to Isle Royale. Crisco's face is chapped since it is cold and there is wind though there is no snow.

We don't go in, don't have a drink, but stand outside instead. This is the place where the schizo guy who held up the bank last winter was shot and killed—taken out—by a SWAT team summoned in from somewhere because God knows we don't have one of our own, much less 911 or Taco Bell. He was taken out through the usual sort of winter blitz. He had hostages. And a bomb strapped to his chest. And a 30.06 on his back. And skis.

I think every place has its own set of deaths. A truck rolls by with oversized wheels and its windshield wipers going and a bumper sticker that says *Mud Bog '97.*

Crisco holds his hands around his ears like he's trying to keep something in. I say "in or out" to Jesse, and gesture toward Crisco's hands, and Jesse takes a flask out from his coat and then we're all taking drinks of shoplifted whiskey—a warm and small reward. Crisco's neck is visible just above the collar of his coat. It is a slice of red flesh in the wind, with acne marks and creases.

We have nothing more to say.

Crisco's bound for it.

Get Started

Sal Luoma's job has nothing to do with ice or verbs, or parallax, or extraction of the wrecks, though in the paper she always reads about those gone through the ice to whatever's after. And when Elizabeth Angstrom doesn't show up for Advanced Chemistry, she can guess why.

It's not as if she's the first woman through the ice, or the last. And it's not like it's some sort of groundbreaking feminist statement that women, too, can drink their stupidity in cups of beer consumed forever after prom, that women, too, can slide on ice and blast through the guardrail in their Fords or Toyotas, and blaze—airborne—into the river, golden and crying and doomed.

It makes her sick.

It makes her think of her estranged daughter who lives in Hubbell, and then makes her think of one-arm Mr. Shutter, the Shop teacher, and then a gleaming table saw, unseen rings around Jupiter, and stars, in that order.

She can't make sense of this thought chain. How did she get from discussing valence electrons to a table saw running at high speed, emitting a high-pitched salty whine, nearing an outstretched wrist like it means to cut right in? There's a connection, she supposes—both are energy, are powerful, are division.

Sal takes it hard when her students die. Harder than most of the teachers at Houghton High School. Harder even than when her daughter got caught and got suspended for stealing the master key for the new high school—she thinks back to that disappointment. Then it makes her feel bad for even twinning in her mind death and suspension, as if they're about the same, approximate. As if Liz's failure to show up for class was related to some hidden discipline, suggested and enforced by a Vice Principal.

They put it in the teacher's manual—that useless, slim, wire-bound thing—*Your students will die on you. Don't get too attached.*

Sal thought that was heartless. *Heartless,* she wrote, in a memo to the Vice Principal, when she first read it, when she had just got this job teaching Chemistry and sometimes Health (inasmuch as they let you teach Health—can't be too specific about sexual awakening or venereal disease in this town; though who are we fooling, she thinks; these kids know a lot already—we are just filling in).

When she got the job, they initially had her monitoring the sixth-graders in Gym as they pelted each other with dodgeballs. She felt inevitable, like she was always somehow meant to be here with these balls in flight, with these bruised and smarting (some of them triumphant) kids. She had to wear a sweatsuit, like her old Gym teacher, Mrs. Sternhagen, wore. She had to buy one since she didn't own one.

The kids always wanted to play a game called Run Until You Die, which Sal didn't know, and refused to let them play because of its title. Why would you want to do that, she asked? They looked sullen and sweaty; they didn't usually say much. So mostly they bowled. With rubber bowling balls specially designed for gym floors and pins guaranteed not to screw up the wax. They learned how to score. This is how you denote a strike, Sal said, drawing an X on a dry erase score sheet she had tacked up on the board. These are important things. This is how you mark a spare, an open frame, a gutter ball.

The Vice Principal, as everybody knows, gets the shit job, and he tells this to himself every day. He is full of the dislike that he's taken in from those around him. His skin has shriveled around the corners of the eyes and mouth. The tightening intensifies the gleam from the pupils and the teeth. He takes this to be a sign of desiccation, a term he never thought he'd apply to himself. Wrinkles sadden him. His heart is not full of desire for discipline at all, he wants to tell each kid they send into his office, but of course he doesn't. That's not the way things are done here in school.

Sal's in the lunchroom. Sixth period is her long lunch thank God yes lord. She's thinking about canceling her afternoon classes (thank God for impromptu Study Hall) and heading up to Kmart to wander around the bathroom aisle. All those products will please and soothe her, will reassure her that things can be clean, and that she is in control. That any stain can be controlled with Formula 409 (cue Beach Boys song) or clear blue Windex that sparkles in its bottle when you hold it up to the sun or to the fluorescent light. That everything is Spic and Span.

What her colleagues don't know is that she collects vintage cleaners. Not out of desire for their chemistry or making (though she thinks about this too), but she likes the look of them like sentries on shelves all around her study. She has over two hundred. She installed the shelves herself—they're very solid, will never spill, except in case of major sonic or seismic boom. It wasn't so difficult, not enough to require, say, the use of power tools or things found in the wood or metal shop.

She doesn't show off this room. It's more a meditation room for herself. She can isolate herself in there among all the bright plastics—and it is increasingly a plastic world, she notes, plastics in fabrics and foods, the technologies of artificial flavoring, of Yellow #5, of methylchloroiso-thiazolinone—and all the labels. There's not too much sun so the colors on the labels don't fade. And if they did, they might be brightened with Clorox 2 with Color Enhancer. They might be polished up, brought back to life.

Perhaps it is unsafe, it occurs to her; maybe all that plastic isn't meant to contain these chemicals for too long. It seems like she should know stuff like this, chemistry and all.

She has this feeling often—that she should be in control of some body of knowledge, that she should be like a reference librarian, filled up to the neck with silver coins and information. At least willing to help.

Thinking about her cleaner collection has distracted her so she doesn't even remember eating the rest of the Healthy Choice rice bowl she brought in and microwaved to life. All wrapped in plastic. In a plastic bowl. Possibly the food coloring or flavoring itself was some polymer.

The Vice Principal thinks to himself how he could have specialized in artificial food flavoring. Now that's a field, he says, a bit disillusioned right now, yes, it's true—he was great in science, thought about graduate school and the life of the mind. He heard about Elizabeth and the after-prom crash, the car through the ice (should they have a moment of silence today announced over the intercom?), and Bernard through the ice further back, on the back of a snowmobile. There are so many gone this way through ice. He resolves to make some sort of promotional material for snowmobile safety (Driver's Ed provides enough graphic gore for would-be invincible auto drivers) to send around the high school: NEVER SNOWMOBILE DRUNK. JUST DON'T DO IT, with a nod to Nike, or maybe that could be transformed into a Nancy Reaganism. He will find students to do presentations. Poster-board triptychs and crappy pastel charts. Spread the gospel. Raise awareness. Maybe they could designate a day, have an assembly. He could make his mark on the school like this.

The high school will be abandoned in less than two years now. The district has just finished constructing new facilities several miles away, and this building—this five-story, old-brick, lead-pipe, and asbestos building—will cease its use at the end of the school year. It will go down to skeleton. A junkyard. Be dismantled like one of the last wooden ships. Or be chalked up to history/TV documentary: This is where Carrie and Bone first met, first kissed; this is where no one said a thing.

There will still be interlopers of course, and the transition between buildings will be slow, but in eighteen months it will be closed. It will be sold around, initially to Pine Manor, an assisted-living home, who will consider refitting it as apartments. That idea will be discarded. Who knows how many kids will throw pipes and rocks and eggs through the windows in the summer, taking out their anger on the architecture. Will break in through the chained and boarded doors, find a way in through a window, and graffiti up the place with spray paint and with chalk. Some of these kids will spray-paint their own names on the inside of the high school and will be caught. Will be fined and prosecuted. Will learn or not learn their necessary lessons.

The high school will be sold and sold and sold until it is slated for demolition. The space will be worth more than the building by then. We might use it as a chemical treatment facility. Or a huge complex designed to store outdated and no-longer-relevant vaccines, medical waste too expensive or dangerous to ship elsewhere or simply discard. All the cadavers, cut apart and discarded. Vivisected on tables for medical students at Gogebic Community College. We can't burn everything.

Will stenographers record the number of first kisses in its halls? The number of cigarettes smoked, crushed out in the bathroom, burned through the clothes, onto the skin? The bruises left behind from older kids who roost on the radiator on cold winter days and charge a buck to piss? Will there be some record, at least, some groove in wax, or magnetic elements aligned on tape, or on some reel? The rings of kids who file into the boys' bathroom on the second floor every year at Sal Luoma's behest to experience electricity firsthand by holding hands and connecting the circuit from one electric hand dryer to the other. Will that be on file?

The gym, which doubles as a lunchroom, with its retractable bleachers that more than one kid has feared being crushed in, will be closed. The often-polished floor torn up. Opportunistic kids will come in with axes and smash it up right before the floor would have been moved to the new building. It's cheaper to move the floor than to buy a new one, have it laid and pressed, and glued down, dried and waxed. But plans will change. Kids with axes. Some unexpected force, some tandem motion in the air.

Sal cancels classes—which she is not supposed to do—and leaves a teacher's aide to run them as an extra Study Hall. Because she needs to get out of there. Because kids can always use more Study Hall. Where things get done, she notes. She's never had to monitor Study Halls, has no idea from her own experience what actually happens there. Kids get jerked off, get bathroom passes, roll cigarettes, throw kisses around. Jab each other with pencils. Fear getting lead poisoning. Perhaps they study, make academic progress.

But Sal doesn't follow the teacher's manual, and she needs the time off. The weight of Liz's absence on her is significant.

The Vice Principal gets a memo about another Shop-class accident. A thumb ground down by a lathe. *Jesus,* he says aloud, and is glad the door's closed, for though he is not religious, others are, and their force in the district is distinct. An Emergency Room visit. He resolves to talk to Mr. Shutter, Shop teacher, master griller, strange man, and a Vietnam vet, or so he claims. The Vice Principal needs to exert some control. He resolves to go down there to the basement, where all the Shop classes are, and where ten years ago, the auto repair classes were, along with mathematics and the remedial students. He resolves to go down there immediately.

Lannie Shutter is rarely surprised. Kids are dumb. The only way, he tells the Vice Principal, to avoid accidents, is to let them use only glue sticks— or, better, paste and tape—or to simply demonstrate and not let them do. But even then, let's say we get some rubber cement: How many of these kids will start huffing it? Eating it? Covering themselves in it and lighting matches as a joke?

But the kids—some of them—enjoy making the pineapple cutting boards so much. They think: cheap Christmas gift. They think: Look what I have made, Dad. They think: Maybe he will like it this year. They go home with a jigsawed piece of pine—something they have made, carved out of the heart of a tree. It would be better, of course, if they were allowed to actually hack down the tree themselves, do the whole shebang. They'd appreciate what it takes to make a uniform slice of wood. But we can't trust them handling axes.

Of course he drills them all the time on safety. Why not to drink. Keep your thumbs to yourselves. No roughhousing in the shop. These machines are not toys. They are powerful and dangerous beasts. Pray to them. Pour a libation from your Coke or the outdated Tab machine upstairs out on the floor before cutting. Wear your goddamned safety goggles.

Why not to smoke. You'll go blind and dumb. Stop, drop, and roll, you kids. Look at this telephone melted in a house fire.

Lannie, mostly referred to as *Mr. Shutter*, is often called up as an example of safety, what with his stump. He thinks sometimes that's why he got the job—he knows all about the Shop teacher clichés, lost digits, etc. It's easy enough to find a guy to play that part.

But look what happens, he says. Look what happens when you tell them not to go around on snowmobiles on thin ice. Do they listen?

No, the Vice Principal says. No, they don't. He understands. Mr. Shutter only has one arm, he notices again, and this is always his problem when talking to Mr. Shutter—he can't forget that absence—either from a circular saw or something, or Vietnam. Everything in Michigan is due to saws or mines or bombs or Vietnam. He can't get past it. He knows other people can, but he just can't. There's something unnatural, unbalanced, like an equation. Something waiting to be righted. Solved.

No one really asks about it. And his kid, little shit Shutter, runs a drug ring that everybody knows about. He's a cat and pot dealer. Everybody knows but Mr. Shutter. Or maybe he knows too.

Lannie runs his hand along the length of one of the table saws.

The Vice Principal climbs the stairs back up to his office. There are a hundred and ten, not including the landings.

Vice Principal. Principal of Vice. Why does everyone spell it PRINCIPLE?

Sal is at Kmart, having hit True Value Hardware and Coast-to-Coast. She's calming now. She buys several bottles of Woolite, because they remind her of her mother. And, by proxy, her mother's car accident, in which she was discovered frozen a day later, covered in Woolite's cool gel. That's an awful image now.

Woolite reminds her of Woolworth's, the kind of store she'd buy cat's-eye marbles at when she was young and would throw them off the bridge. Her mother would buy her bags and bags of marbles every year—that was all she wanted—and Sal would throw them off the Lift Bridge into the Portage Canal. She wonders how many marbles there are down there. Do they all collect to the same place? Is there some submerged marble pot that a diver might find down there with all her marbles and those of other kids who had either lost their parents or who had not. Who had maybe just seen her hucking marbles as far out as she could into the water. Who were inspired; who followed this example.

She bets there is a ton of marbles scattered down there somewhere.

Sal would love to be a diver, sleek in a wetsuit. Going under the water. Exploring the wrecks. Left alone in the element.

She wonders who came up with marbles, why or how they're made.

She played marbles with her friend Jerry, who had some steelies as big as a fist, which were nearly impossible to play with being heavy and huge, but were so cool. They played one time for keepsies—whoever won would keep both marbles—and she lost, and Jerry kept his huge steelies. And she felt bad, but not as bad as if she'd won, because they weren't hers to start with.

Those must not have been marbles but bearings for trains or huge tractors, semitrucks or other big, incomprehensible machines.

The Vice Principal knows more than he lets on.

This is what Vice Principals do, he thinks. It's his job to know, to have informants in the student body. He tapes conversations in the bathrooms. It's illegal, sure, but at least this way he knows. Someone has to know. The Principal has better things to do. Curricula and the superintendent and such.

He knows how many of the girls are pregnant (four).

He knows who's responsible.

He thinks of the end of the day which is approaching.

He stops by the Emergency Room to check on the thumb-lathed kid. He seems to be okay. No permanent disfigurement. He leaves a card he bought downtown with signatures of the secretaries in the office. On his way out, he's not sure why he did that.

He has a few minutes, so he goes down to the bridge and walks out on the lower level by the tower where there are strobe lights at night up there—it's like there's a party going on—or else it keeps the bats away, or warns planes, or something. He throws some loose change into what would be water in the summer. And is water, now, just cold enough so it's frozen. Nickels skitter on the cool floor.

The water's gray where you can see it looming through the ice. The ice is fissured. There's a large black mark out in its middle. He thinks for a second that it's in the shape of a snowmobile, or a car, or the body of a boy.

Sal is in the Kmart bathroom, where it warns: "Shoplifting is not a prank or a joke. You will be prosecuted." She hears a girl in the next stall working on some plastic packaging. This is a shoplifting taking place, she thinks, and wonders if she should tell someone, if the authorities should be informed. She hears a man crying through the wall. You can tell it's a man by the tenor of the sobs. It's always worse when men cry. Unattractive. Really ugly. The girl in the next stall gets up and flushes, then is gone. Sal wonders if the sign was meant for her, if she would be prosecuted. She wonders if Kmart sells marbles.

Lannie Shutter contemplates the pitch of the floor that angles down to the drain. There are still spots of blood or paint near that drain. Who knew a lathe could do that to a kid? He wasn't watching. Wonders what the kid was doing. He can see that anything dropped in the shop would eventually make its way to the drain, unless blockaded by another object. He wonders if this is intentional, if the makers of the shop figured on blood being spilled, on glass eyes being dropped, on screws or nails falling to the floor. Everything converges at the drain. This makes him feel good about things again. He is sure that his kid, the shit, is doing something wrong, but thinks that he'll get redirected by some force, some simple machine, some inclined plane or block and tackle. He cleans the saw blades. Everybody ends up in the right place.

The Vice Principal is in a dead-wall reverie, staring blankly at the ceramic wall tiles. Counting them. He's in his office. Making Calculations. Doing Important Work. He is Not To Be Disturbed, nor Disrobed. This is how he amuses himself.

He listens to some ghetto rap—offensive enough that he confiscated a CD from that Jesse kid a week ago. Everyone listens to this stuff now. He listens to the samples constructed over beats, and words over all of it. It's angry. He can see the attraction. He holds his hand to the light. Drives a tack in his palm. It hurts. The Vice Principal appreciates the singular fact of this pain.

Sal is out. The sky is darkening. It's not chook-cold, or *took-cold* as they say in Canada after their strange name for those Finnish winter caps they wear tugged over their ears. Or is it *toque,* she wonders? It is, though, cold enough so driving's treacherous (more treacherous than usual). Oh Liz, Liz. A television's on in someone's car. She's stopped at one of the few lights in town and this guy's got a TV in his car. Imagine that. There is the news, but she can't hear anything. Only sees the lighted collection of pixels—are they pixels, anyhow? is that the term?—that make up his false jaw and creased forehead. It is very colorful and she is very tired. There is an accident up ahead. She sees it as traffic begins to trickle forward underneath the light. From below—she's looking up, not at the road— you can't tell what light is what. Is it red or green?

Pay attention, Sal. You know how these pileups get started.

Instructions
for Divers:
On Retrieval

D iver down, you get the gruesome task of following the canal floor to come upon the body. Others have charted the approximate speed from the witnesses who saw it happen, the angle of submersion judging by the cracks that radiated out from the hole in the ice. You have the figures and follow the line down. Your wife is in the house and you do not miss her. Not when underwater. You do not miss your kids of three and six whom you have difficulty dealing with. You can't understand sometimes their misbehavior and wonderment at the world. This is what you do—you're mostly a recreational summer diver exploring the many shallow lake wrecks in the waterways. But in the winter, you're needed in this other way, to descend, fully-insulated, through the ice, tied up with line to assure your safe return to the surface. You hold the line as you move downstream. Sometimes you contemplate cutting it and letting it float back up. You contemplate the dismay above, like when you were little and would wish for your death so you could attend the funeral and watch all your family crying.

A little light filters through the ice in several spots. It looks weaker from below than from above. Kaleidoscopic. You are equipped with underwater beams. A Kodak underwater camera to document your find. You know the currents, where they take everything that descends. You carry weights to ensure your travel along the lake floor. It's like the moon in that way. Just as easily you could jump up and carry a hundred, or a thousand feet down the canal. Very few will ever witness this. A half-mile downstream you find the wreck among maybe forty old desiccated machines. This is the spot at which most wrecks eventually arrive. Something about the way the current moves—and though a snowmobile is weighty, the water does not stop its motion, and learns to move it, solves the problem, eventually has its way. This is the awful part. You need to note—you know—the license number. Confirm. You need to tag it with the orange tape that reminds you of how the police mark the antennae of cars buried in the ditch. Take a couple photos from alternating angles.

Attach the body to hooks with which you are equipped. You are always very well-equipped. It is a man. It is usually a man. Though there are exceptions. He is brightly colored, silent. You don't relate this find to your family in the world above. When they ask you how it went, what it is you do, exactly, you will evade their query. You must not answer conclusively. You are the sole proprietor of this brief grief. You know the stories about the monks who flail themselves, as if to consume a finite pint of suffering, so the millers, the bakers, the meat-cutters and drink-pourers, the childcare workers, and the street snow-cleaners will have less than half their share. You think of yourself like this because it is all you can do to keep it in while you tug the line twice and it is reeled back up. You never surface with the body. You prefer to stay below a little longer. The water's cold but through the insulation you can barely feel it. Your body temperature drops every minute you stay. Still you cannot bear the surfacing until the body has been drawn away, until you've seen the flashing lights of the funeral home minivan move away—they are just barely visible through the ice—and the dead one is carted back to those whose task is the sprucing up of skin and smile.

Subtraction Is the Only
Worthwhile Operation

This story is a reflex against grief: it is seen through Sunday glass or on TV, is watched from outside, without sound. Is found scratched in the cover of an old Webster's with a knife or with another semisharp instrument, like a compass or an edge of glass. Is buried underneath the woodshed with the words where you once promised your friend Jesse you'd change his sex with a tampon and couldn't do it. Is black mark on paper, an X, a target on a map. Specifies where the old words are, the ones that you're not allowed upon penalty of death to use or even look at. Why bury words in bags. Why bury variables in algebra. Why solve for X or Y. Why balance this equation. Why story problems, codes, or mounds of equations, parametric. Why all this snow coming—why does snow erase or hide? Is hide an abstraction like subtraction? Why tell stories underneath the fire to your brother who doesn't often speak. Why drive him anywhere or reminisce about your mother—gone long for the season, gone with the benevolent weather and the crystal beauty and the reflections in the lake. Gone with the sky lights and fire from distant stars. Gone with invisible breath mingling in air, gone like walking without a trace. She is line noise, clipping in to junction boxes. She is interference, underlying every conversation you have with what's left of your extended family. She is your father insomuch as your father is not himself but words in the night air encoded in shortwave radio hand-me-downs. She is Orpheus crossing the International Bridge into Canada in a hearse. She is going to bring you something back. She is going to mine the amethyst from the quarry and bring you back something beautiful and precious. She is answer and solution, unknown moan and ampersand. She connects your calls that stretch overseas to radio stations where you call in Long Distance Dedications to Liz, stations that would never make it in the air to Upper Michigan. Stations that she will never hear. This is acting out a role a part a portion of a story, a product of long lust kept under glass and in the low-heat oven. This is blackened, baked, a neck connecting the voice to the lung. A larynx always getting shorter. The highway dashes as they go by in your father's car as you're crossing into Canada on the bridge in high winds. He tells you and your brother about the Yugo that was blown off the bridge in these same high winds on the way to Canada, and you imagine an identical but drowned brother at the bottom of the lake below glass, and your identical, drowned self, and a locked safe in the back of the car, locked with the words inside that you can never bring yourself to find or say.

Dream Obits
for Carrie H.

Though we were not friends.

Though you were an emblem of our town's loss, of our friend Crisco's loss.

Though you were meant in an awful way for Bone that storm that frozen bog.

Though those who knew you well couldn't stop it.

Though this was not exactly accident.

Though your story (and not others) would gather sensation, AP news release, mentions on the news all the way to Canada, the reporters coming in to feed.

Though your story would be a *story*—the murdered girl. The loveliness.

The *Twin Peaks* obvious analogy. The made-for-TV movie. The perfect documentary in the making.

Though there is no mystery there how it happened.

Though you were our babysitter.

Though you were a high-achiever, one of those girls bound for eternal honor roll and Ph.D. if nothing got to you before.

Though in school you were obsessed with mathematics, with patterns in the carpet, on the ceiling, in the weather, in the bathroom stalls.

Though you never saw it coming when it came.

Though we think of you out at the breakers, where the canal opens out into the Lake, where the waves are greatest and the land divides itself in two.

Though we know that in your way you loved him, even as he undid you.

Though we think of you in front of fires out at the breakers, transfixed by the motion of the flames, some order you saw in there.

Though those who didn't know you think of you as Girl Who Was Murdered, as Tragic Girl, as Story, as Warning Beacon.

Though in our dreams we always see you in red.

Though in our dreams we always see you smiling in Study Hall, arm crooked over a marked-up Geometry text.

Though we see you as Girl Who Was Well-Loved.

Though we think of you as to be desired (because now you're scarce).

Though we think of you in terms of economics, of demand for exceeding supply.

Though we think increasingly of you in metaphor, as metaphor.

Though you were not finally meant for us.

Though finally you were meant for something else and out of here.

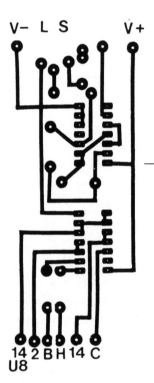

Dear, I know that absence is an abscess

We Are Going to
See the Oracle of
Apollo in Tapiola,
Michigan

It's true that she stays in the back of the store: a half-diner/half-gas station that's reputed to be one of the true sources of pornography in Upper Michigan and is definitely a reliable bait shop. It is true that she is only here one month each year, right after the Fourth of July when all the fireworks have been disposed of in the trash, or in the grass, or in the lake. It is true that I am going to see her with Liz my X my alphabet in the passenger seat. We are listening to New Order which excites the blood in the way that summer does when it comes unexpectedly and lasts for at least a day. It is true that it is cold here most of the time, even through the summer, the wind kicking through the trees like a vandal like a pirate on gunwales on the plank. It is true that this is just after Liz moved here, in a way replacing Caroline, who was Canadian and the obsession of all the boys, who went Christian and set fire to all her tapes (a spiritual coming-out party to which we were all invited), who moved away without word or note or lipstick trace or forwarding address. It is true there are things I feel for Liz that I have not told her about being just friends or the else that is fire that may be the kind of fire I want. It is too true that we are quiet in the car.

I do not know that Liz will soon be gone, that she will be up and packed and trussed and sunk and gone.

The radio in my car doesn't work that well so we can't hear that well.

The sun is up but hazy and I look over at her who is like an element on the periodic table, a symbol an enigma sign of light. Liz who must be solved for. Liz who collected architectural drawings, stole them from the public library in town where they keep them under glass, or the county courthouse where they keep a plan of every building that is made. Liz who sends me invisible ink notes.

My brother is at home and I do not think about him now. He is not with me like a ghost or a dedication on the radio that finds you wherever you can go to or get out from.

It is true that I have questions for the Oracle, like how to get the Playboy channel, or will the school burn down to cinder, char in Fall.

It is true I have more important questions about my mother or the weather.

I ask Liz what her questions are for the Oracle but she won't tell me. She doesn't ask me what are mine.

We hear bottle rockets firing in the sky. They are leftover from the Fourth.

I don't tell her that we used to fire the rockets at houses from PVC pipes turned into homemade bazookas. I don't tell her that my brother almost lost his hearing when one misfired, how those things are cheap and unreliable, how they can't be trusted, but they do the most wonderful and explosive things.

The wind is in our hair because my back windows do not fully close.

We are in my father's Aerostar.

Everyone I know has a minivan.

Liz does not seem impressed with it. She does not seem impressed by much.

She doesn't ask about my brother's arms, which I am thankful for. I try to keep him secret since there is no satisfaction there.

In Algebra we always had to solve for X.

2 / We Are Still Going to See the Oracle of Apollo in Tapiola, Michigan

Liz's hair reminds me of paramecia with their tiny microfingers that move them in the ooze. I do not tell her this. We are coming up through the valley that my family used to drive through on the way to Ironwood where the ski slopes are, where the car dealerships are, where I would eventually be arrested for leaving the scene of an accident where I hit a gas pump, freaked, and fled. We are coming up through the valley in which my dad would always sing "Down in the Valley" when we still drove through here as a family on the way to recreation, the Porcupine Mountains or the state line that leads to Wisconsin, land of more snow and beer and cheese. We are coming up through the valley that I have memories of. Liz and I are in the valley and we are coming up the other side like we were in Montana next to some great crest.

We talk of Florida, the postcards we get from relatives who've visited or moved there. We talk about all the oranges that are huge and the futuristic ball of Epcot Center that I've always wanted to visit but never have.

We are going to see the Oracle who will tell us we must go to Paulding to see the Mysterious and Possibly Awful Light. This is what we think—that this trip will snowball and soon we will be bound to visit all the sites of strangeness in Michigan. Our parents will never miss us. At least mine will not, I suspect.

Liz taunts truckers on the CB which is beautiful, which is funny, which might be dangerous like in the movies or in the stories you hear about taunting truckers, which you are not supposed to do and live, and which we do. Liz my elevation. Liz my hatchet man.

3 / You Cannot Stop Us; Yes We Are Still Going

Besides electricity, other things can move us. Gasoline for one, or loyalty, or fire. Fire that comes from anything that is a burst a birth a burning bush that will soon go out in snow. Fire that is a way of loving property. Fire that is my cousin Ben when he stayed with us, out until too late doing God Knows What in Michigan then returning with his boots loud on the floor of the house. Fire that is my mother's trail to Canada and to all the glory roadside sites of hugeness in America in North America in the North. Fire that is her that is aurora in the sky. I have told Liz some of this, a little bit at a time. She knows what fire is to me. She bought me gasoline for my last birthday, and rags, and matches. Fire that is the opposite of cold that means never freezing, that means combustion, spontaneity, and marshmallows skewered on sticks, turning black. Besides electricity, the thought of the humongous fungus moves us like a magnet. The thought of the Paulding Light that rocks back and forth in the distance just outside of Paulding which is buried in the woods which is an hour and a half from the hills that are made of mines in the Keweenaw Peninsula, which is an hour and a half from the canal that cuts the Peninsula in half, which is an hour and a half from the sliced thumb of land that juts out into Lake Superior like a missed note does in a song and wrecks it like a boat on rocks. The thought of the fungus is a magnet which is a field which electricity creates. My mother is a field which electricity creates, which keeps me, satellite, in place. Which keeps me in the car with Liz on our way to Tapiola.

4 / Onward to the Oracle

Tapiola is not so far away as this. It is not the ornate crown of the Mediterranean. It is not the cities they show on Canadian TV that come over the lake at night to us. It is not the glittering office towers of Sault Ste. Marie, Canada, as seen across the international waters, as seen across a year of fire and ears suspended in jars, cupped to the ground.

Tapiola is where Liz and I will find an answer to this story, where Liz and I will kick the screen door in on the place where the Oracle is in the back. Where Liz and I will not leave until we are satisfied. Where Liz and I will never be satisfied, I know, because what will she—the Oracle— really have to say that I don't know already: that Liz will leave like summer does, that my brother has no answers for his arms, his aphasia, for where his plate should go on the counter when he's done with it. That this story is a story of the body of the heart of the left atrium, the ballroom where prom will eventually be held. That though there is still ore in the ground, we have mined the hills to the point where any further excavation will collapse the thing, even a hundred people jumping up and down simultaneously to counteract the Chinese kids who are—in mass—trying to force the earth's orbit to change by jumping on the other side of the globe.

This is what our Science teachers sell us to get us to go outside and jump as a class, as a whole white shining class who will not all—of course—graduate, a class who will lose half to moving costs or crime, or to weather or sickness, barn collapse, misguided amputations, or to dropping out and, frustrated, frequenting bars. This is what our Science teachers tell us to do, but what they do not tell us is this: Our jumping could collapse the shafts and close the mine that is like a trachea, that is the only reason a generation had for settling here, that is the only thing that has brought Liz, with her fascination with the architectures of the cities, the architecture of the towns vacated to ghosts, buried in the woods, and the architecture of the mines that reminds me of heartworms burrowing through the organs of a pet who is loved, who is too far gone to care.

5 / The Oracle of Apollo in Tapiola Will Punctuate Our Sentences With Groans and Fill in All Our Deepest Holes With Putty Like a Dentist Would That Will Harden and Protect Us Permanently From Harm

We have stopped talking, Liz and I, because we are almost there, and we have our own things to think about.

Tapiola doesn't have any outskirts, exactly, being small, so we go right from the woods through the population sign into the town and to the store that is the diner that is the place where the Oracle will tell us Truths and that is the place where we can maybe grab a bite before returning or going somewhere else.

Everything is run-down and beautiful. The Tapiola General Store that is the Tapiola Diner has these old pillars out front like Rome like Greece like some architectural culture, except that these are spray-painted with slogans from local high school kids and left here for character, for show. These pillars support nothing. They just stand at the front of the store, which is where we pull in, which is where we kick up dust since we have left the asphalt that kept all the dust and all the forest away.

Liz gets out first.

There is not much light left.

The store is open, so we go in.

It has no door.

There is an array of bait in tubs and tanks.

There is a counter area and several booths that seem to me like the traps some people put out to catch bears or wolves, but that catch mostly dogs and often maim them.

There is a very little light coming from a chandelier above.

I imagine this is quite a scene.

We tell the guy behind the counter who may be a relative of mine or Liz's that we are here to see the Oracle. He thinks this is Hilarious. He laughs. He has fine white teeth that gleam like in commercials.

He says *Go straight through to the back through both sets of doors that are hard to open but you look like a strong guy,* is what he says.

Which is what we do.

No one is there.

It is cold and there is a lot of ice.

I think we are in a freezer, is what I say to Liz.

Isn't it a pity, the Oracle says when she comes in. She looks about fifteen.

I ask her what she means.

There is a radio stating numbers—one-one-seven, one-one-nine-four—that she has her ear cocked toward. Another shortwave radio spills weather information. Yet another radio just hushes static. There is an old boat radio and barometer saying something in another language.

I will not tell you what she says to Liz or what she says to me.

It is true we find out nothing here.

Regardless, Liz is doomed and beautiful, maybe one because of the other, and it is cold, and I suppose I am in love, which is too bad. We will get a meal in Tapiola, battered, fried, and better than we expected, leaving us full and gassy. It is all we can honestly ask for before we leave and get back in the Aerostar, where the radio will play us some songs that mean a lot, that we understand.

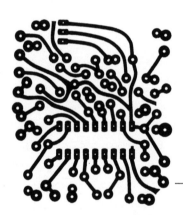

———————— *Dear, wish you were here with me in sun and warmer air*

To Reduce
Your Likelihood
of Murder

Do not go outside. Do not go outside, on dates, or to the store, alone. Do not go on dates with men. Do not go on dates with men who drive. Do not drive yourself to dates, because that may anger the man you are dating who may wonder if you're too good to step foot in his new custom chrome *baby-baby* car. Do not date men who sit in or lean on cars. Do not sit in cars or sprawl yourself against the seat, or lean up against the metal skin of the door while you are being kissed. Do not date at night. Do not walk at night. Do not walk at night alone. Do not be alone. Walk with a girlfriend or someone else. A man you trust? Do not spend time with men, men friends, or boys. Do not spend time with any kind of men at all. Do not spend time with friends at all. Most women are killed by someone they know. Most women are killed by someone they know intimately.

Install alarm systems on every window, every doorway in your house. Better, do not live in a house. Go apartment. Go co-op. Go someplace where you can be heard, where someone can hear you scream. Do not venture out in public (at night, alone). Do not stay at home. Do not wear black. Do not wear the dress your boyfriend likes so much. Do not date your boyfriend whom you like so much. Do not like so much. Do not say *like* so much. Everyone is a potential murderer. And murderee. You are the murderee. You are single, seventeen, and thin. You are a thing made for television, for the nights of drama crime. Do not watch crime shows on TV or DVD. Do not open the door for anyone. Do not tell your mother that you don't know when you'll be back. Do not frustrate. Do not comply. You must lie somewhere in-between.

Do not sleep deeply.

Do carry mace, or pepper spray, or a bowie knife. Do carry guns if you can get them. A crossbow. A blowgun. Do subscribe to the *Shotgun News* and carry it wherever you go. It will be a totem, will keep you safe from harm. Armor yourself: plate mail, chain mail, studded leather armor. Helms and chain-link gloves. Keep away from the windows at all times. You must be surprising: Always travel in a crowd, in a cloud of smoke. Cover all your tracks. Keep an eye behind. Switch cabs. Duck into dead-end streets and wait for cars to pass.

Still you will be killed. You're born for it. Your life is a tree meant to be torn apart by weather and electricity.

Freda
Thinks Spring

Rob and Freda sit in front of a pyramid of a hundred-and-twelve shot glasses with logos from every NFL team. The weather report on the radio says don't go out tonight, it's just not worth it. Eight inches of snow at Houghton County airport in Calumet and counting. Freda cracks the blinds and sees that there's no sign of it stopping. She wishes the TV still worked, but it died two weeks ago in a power surge from a storm. There's a half-empty bottle of shitty vodka in the fridge along with some old red wine which isn't nearly as good as the advertisement said.

Rob's eyes are closed as she looks at him, sniffs the air, looks at the grandfather clock—her father's—and it chimes eight times, slowly. She stands up and goes to the silverware drawer, takes out a pack of playing cards, sits back down, and begins to count. They were all there last night, but she knows Rob, so like his brother Bone, who has a certain magnetism that Rob lacks but who also frightens her quite more than Rob; she knows both like to steal the queen of clubs.

Freda plays solitaire, making seven neat stacks, turning the top cards over with her hand. She can tell all the jacks because they're dogeared, but it's fun to play anyhow. Her wrists are thin and birdlike; they seem to be something apart from the rest of her body as she watches her fingers manipulate the cards, flipping, moving, and stacking, starting a clubs pile with the ace.

Rob stands and goes over to the couch, flops down on his stomach, without opening his eyes. It's darker there. The light in the living room is on hiatus right now, he's said. She kind of likes it that way. It lends the room a weirdness. The tractor pictures on the wall, and the one of the green John Deere riding lawnmower, turn deeper shades, become sinister. She looks at Rob's form, his stomach—wide and hairless like his brother's, like an open, snowed-in field—moving slowly, raising and lowering his back.

Freda makes a decision. "Let's go driving, honey." Her voice reaches the end of the room and stops, turns around, sits down. "Hey, sweets?" The question reclines, brings out the footrest on the used La-Z-Boy.

The humidifier turns on to fill the silence, hums and blows warm, moist air into the room. It waits and shuts off. The shadows shift and shift back.

Freda gets up and walks to the rubber doormat, puts on her boots. They're cold. She starts to lace them up. "Hello? Are you coming?"

"You go."

She brings the strings around the back and ties tight bows in the front. She reaches for her heavy jacket. The keys jingle quietly in the pocket. She grabs his hat and pulls it over her hair. "I'll be back, then."

The door opens and closes. Chilly air rushes in. Rob shifts positions, gropes for a terry-cloth towel, throws it over his feet.

Outside, Freda's kicking at big chunks of snow, smashing them on the way to the truck. She hopes it starts. She's pretty sure it will.

The snow falls quietly, more silently than she thought. She stops walking and listens. It's so much quieter out here, she thinks, like there's a huge cone of hush all around her. Nothing moves except the snow. It comes down so slowly that when she forgets her boots and the ground, it seems like she's going up. It floats lazily through the glow of the streetlight, making the illuminated area almost solid.

There's so much space here, but it's beautiful, not like inside. The air in there's too old and hard, lonely but refusing to admit it. Here it's shocking, cold, but so soft. It reminds her of church when she was young. The snow alighting on her nose seems warm. Catching a flake on her tongue, it's salty. Like a piece of warm dirt. Or dust from somewhere way up there, who knows how high, from the top of Quincy Hill maybe, floating down across the canal, gaining speed, picking up precipitation, to her. Or maybe it's from somewhere around the world.

She decides to pass the truck and walk down toward the wide canal. She's careful where her feet go because a slip could be ugly out here alone. No one would come out in this weather to find her, ankle twisted and swelling, gasping tiny puffs of hot air into the night.

It's a perfect kind of silence. So much snow coming down. She knows this as she gets down the trail to the shore, holding onto familiar trees on the way since the path is treacherous with the only light filtering through the snow from the high white moon. Birch, birch, blue spruce, birch.

The woods fall away and she's out on the beach. The water isn't frozen over yet, so it laps quietly as it swallows the snow. She sits down, her butt slowly understanding the cold, cell by cell.

There was a time when she hated the snow, when her brothers would push her face down in gritty city snow, filled with tiny jagged rocks. They'd laugh and leave her to get up, clean the cuts, cuts so small she couldn't see them, except when she pressed her fingers to her face and felt a drop of blood slip out, smear in a circle on her fingertip. She'd lick the finger with her hot tongue. As she got older and taller, she grew to know the taste.

Big 32

210 — true boiling point of water at this altitude in this climate in this place in the summer underneath the summer heart and heat, given the mineral residue from the mines and other impurities that have made it into the water, and given the general resistance of the people this far North to drinking water straight without fizz, a lime, or an alcoholic spike. Drink up. You find fish floating gut-up in some of the lakes. Come out and grab them with your hands. Take them home and clean them up; cut out the tumors and they're fine to eat. Though still, in Harriet's opinion, an unacceptable risk. Some things are worth your life and other things are not.

184 — temperature of sparks caused by the plow blade on winter pavement after cutting through the epidermis of snow; Harriet always felt it was like the guys who fired off bottle rockets and roman candles on the Fourth while she ate fried fish: greasy, good, both the boys (though just for a while) and definitely the fish. Liz and Harriet would pick up these kinds of boys some summer nights, do their cool-girl smoking thing in the Subway parking lot as the leftover gunpowder haze settled around them like a shawl. Liz and Harriet in that shawl together, boys outside. Harriet more coy, all smolder, no flare; Liz all burn, a bright and flying thing, a beacon.

184 — sparks don't stay at this temperature for long. They're like birds moving swiftly South for winter. Or atoms dying. A flake of dandruff descending to the floor at the end of an aborted date.

114 — when she exfoliates her skin by rubbing quickly, this is how hot it gets.

106 — as high as her body temperature has ever gotten; scared her father sick what with her mother gone a month before and Harriet bedridden and brow hot as a wake-up airplane towel; she made it to the Emergency Room and they managed to bring it down with ice and medication; temperature she has tattooed on her lower back as her breaking point. The tattoo that she showed to Liz just after having it done at the only tattoo place in town. Liz surprised, for once a step behind—like in a daze. Even briefly jealous, Liz. Temperature of no small excitement.

97 — to break the jump between her breaking point and a pleasant summer evening. It rarely gets above this temp. in the Northern end of Michigan, but when it does she has her work to do: the tar and asphalt patches she does on her sections of road (yes she has responsibilities even in the summer that can usually be defined as *lack of snow*, of ice, of good reasons for accidents) are not made for temperatures this high, since studies show it rarely gets this hot and studies show it's cheaper to use cheaper patching materials and have to patch more often than it would be to use the premium patching quick-dry asphalt.

84 — fire danger changes from *high* to *medium*, assuming the humidity remains the same. Memory of Liz glimpsed at night in the parking lot, sharing a beer with Bone Lumberg, that dark spot, that nothingness. (This memory well before Bone and Carrie—a sort of early murder prototype—but without that fit, that spark and blaze.) Memory of Liz this time gone solo.

71 — is about as good as it gets up in Michigan on summer nights when Harriet is mostly unemployed, watching *Twin Peaks* or reading, formerly drinking with Liz before the minor snub, the prom, the X, the accident, the bleak and blackness after, dreaming of inevitable winter overtime checks and the sparklight of plow blade on concrete or the regular geometry of a graded gravel road.

65 — Harriet's grandparents keep the house this temperature in the winter, which is much too cold and requires the wearing of sweaters, insulation by afghan and blanket, and alcohol infusions. Sometimes she wears her snowmobile mittens and full snowplow regalia at dinner to make her point, which entertains but does no good. Harriet promises herself she'll host Christmas next year so she can jack it up.

58 — four deaths in Harriet's family occurred at this temperature— summer falls to throat cancer, emphysema, a heart attack, and complications after surgery to remove a lump from the upper arm. Liz said that, given this, this temperature is bad news for H. and anyone H. knows. Liz said *God, Harriet, I think you're dangerous.* Harriet flushed at this declaration, its maybe-irony. She stays away from the phone until the sun has plunged below the lip of the world and the air cools. During these hours, Liz knew not to call, but show up unannounced instead.

57 — when the temperature gets this cold or below, she knows—or used to know, until a year ago—she's safe from loss.

55 — is unseasonably nice for Michigan between the poles of Halloween and Easter; means either no work for H. or more trouble when the temperature spikes up this high for a day, prompting the melt and rush, unfreezing pipes, because it's always followed by a dive back down and pipes splitting like cooking sausage and the shriek of copper tubing giving way. Fifty-five degrees in summer means a chilly night, no work of course since no snow, which means relief and nights spent reading Chandler, Dashiell Hammett, or James M. Cain, nights embedded in the motions of the plot like a car along a mountain road with snow gusting from behind.

54 — after the spring thaw and the snow has melted from the roads, it's time to take note of the cracks budding in the pavement—those will take some care when the rain stops to cover over. Harriet attends to her road like a surgeon without the sense of crushing responsibility she knows the most human of them must feel. The asphalt patching—not just the clearing of the snow—is her job. Like a naughty, flat black devil baby.

49 — the temperature on the bus she used to take to school with Liz listening to crap 80s radio like "I Love a Rainy Night" by whoever the hell sang that, when she used to carve the initials of her and Liz and various boys into the backs of seats to commemorate their love forever. Temperature at which she got her bus privileges revoked and had to get her dad to drive her to school, which meant breakfasts at McDonalds, sausage & egg McMuffins, and the sight of her dad through coffee steam like a winter storm.

46 — the roads sometimes steam at this temperature after the rain has passed and the day is starting up; a small pleasure, difficult to share since it vanishes so early.

44 — breath will steam in air; Harriet's brother becomes a dragon, goes Godzilla, stomping towns. Gusts of germ-laden breath.

43 — she begins to feel like she's on a slide toward winter, no getting off. When she was young Harriet would want to stay in the middle of the slide. She'd hold her feet against the sides and make the rubber scream. She'd cause huge pileups on the playground or when her parents took her to theme parks with the rides and kids with their faces full of spun pink candy.

42 — Harriet begins to watch the sky for signs of clouds or precipitation; even when she's out for mediocre Italian food she's glancing furtively at the coats of customers as they come in for evidence of snow (and the ruination of another nice evening out with one of many boys). Sits by the window if she can help it, or at least sits close enough to the door. It feels like in her life she is always by the door.

41 — when it hits this temperature, 41-cent coffees from 41 Lumber which is on her road section, though not quality coffee (need it even be said?), nor good conversation. But coffee is an inoculation against the coming cold. Also the number of the highway that begins a half-hour north of her and runs down to the television heat dream that is Miami, a sunlamp in her mind.

40 — temp. at which Harriet always thought she would be proposed to, whenever that would happen, it would be outdoors, their breath intermingling in the air before the kiss would bring on a more pleasing and intimate contact; yes sounds so lovely at this temperature, and even *I'm just not sure* won't sound like a rebuff, but a temporary hesitation, an invitation for more: even Liz agreed (said *yes* when pressed) when H. told her this. (Liz not meant, she thought, for married life. Liz unbound, like a flashlight beam coming through your finger skin, regardless.) It's still not so cool that the heart can tell, but cold enough to give the impression of colder days to come.

39 — how cold it is in the mine in which her father's father worked and died from soot and long days without light.

37.5 — at this temperature, the yearly tally of accidents due officially to inclement weather begins. This tally will only grow and grow.

36 — how cold it has to be for the mine canaries to die and sometimes cause a panic with the miners running, fearing gas; of course they don't use mine canaries anymore, do they?

35 — the road needs salt, so now she's like a nurse, administering a needle to the flat black tarry patient. Would that she had been a nurse and on the scene when she was necessary. Would that Liz had not gone through the guardrail (and on to what was beyond for her) on Harriet's stretch of road—this coincidence at the least a difficulty in her mind, maybe something unforgivable and worse.

33–30 — range of snowball-packing temperatures for Timothy who is still young enough to want to throw the hardest iceball he can find at windows in the neighborhood. Always gives you sticky snow that won't be snow for too much longer, that might melt down to ground or translate to chilly bruises on a face. Telephone poles losing all the winter ice, that information carried within the lines somehow freer and faster-moving, those voices coded as electrical pulses less encumbered, breathing easier, more honestly.

32 — the big one, means death to some, the annual accumulation of the bodies in the morgue then to the mortuary then to the mausoleum—going through the gates of all those *M*s on their way to come-spring burial.

32 — also tattooed on her back, right below, a spot only four people have ever seen (after the second tattoo), and on which none have failed to remark. Liz of course was one of them, though much later, when she was being stalked and would stay some nights at Harriet's, when she would get those calls and go on those aimless drives with him, listening to New Order, just solo Liz and him (were they friends, what does that mean?), then she would come back to Harriet's to spend the nights. These nights spent drinking themselves into a haze, some nights spent in other, better ways. Tattoos sometimes freak men out. Tattooed numbers always freak men out. One more good reason to have them, and have them hidden. Control your circumstances. Control your body.

28 — temp. at which salted roads used to ice, before they invented the modern kind of chemical salt.

26.6 — temperature of the present tense, the second anniversary of Liz through the ice. When you have a thermometer accurate to the tenths of degrees, you can be more serious about weather.

26 — salt time for the road which means going to the monster set of white salt breasts jutting up underneath the bridge with their metal silo bra. It entertains her.

23 — temperature at which Liz's breath was memorialized on glass in Harriet's parents' house during the last-minute pre-prom freeze just before her passing. Temperature at which *Liz ♥ Harriet* was written. Temperature at which Harriet wished she had removed the pane and kept it in her freezer like a trophy bass or hunted winter remnant meat. Like she could have had it taxidermied, mounted on the wall.

21 — consider the numbers: At least two hundred in the hospital every winter from catastrophe traffic; an average of thirty die. Add those who lose it to exposure like Harriet's uncle who got drunk and couldn't make it back to the warm recliner and his coffee left on the plate to boil down to caffeinated tar. Add those to the nightly news death ticker, and other ways to go.

20 — temperature at which salted roads will ice, no matter what you do.

18 — an unexpected September plunge brings her out of the summer reading in her car to troll her section of the highway for danger spots and thoughts of ice. No precipitation spotted for the evening, but she can feel it in her scapula which rings the neck with its tiny pain bell.

14 — temperature at which it does no good to scrape or chop the ice away.

5 — degrees by which the Houghton National Bank time and temp. sign is always off; it's impossible for Harriet to come to terms with this, considering so much of her life is bound by time and temperature. How much effort would it really take to fix?

3 — sex by now is really a chore unless you've got things insulated well.

0 — this low means the mayor considers canceling schools, though without heavy winds and blowing snow (meaning low visibility), it's an iffy call. Some people feel a sense of pride in never closing schools.

-9 — the plow itself can barely keep warm when it's this cold, so she bought electric socks from Kmart that don't work worth a quarter of a shit—the single wire snaking through the fabric burns her skin while the rest stays cold and gray as the day. Good concept though an underwhelming execution. Mark those for a return if she could only find the receipt.

-10 — in Harriet's opinion, this is shitkicking illegal cold.

-11 — tears freeze complete; nosehairs froze twenty degrees ago; so crying will get you nowhere, like her dad's dead dad used to say.

-16 — if it stays this cold for long the body will cease its moaning and desist, finally relax into the stiffness and the air and silence, cease steaming, cease all the cogitation, the deeper sense of culpability, of—let's make it tire-bald, slippery as black ice spread across a road—guilt, or maybe of forgiveness, one of the other signs of life.

-19 — coldest recent day that she can remember, aside from the windchill factor which the meteorologists say makes it seem so much worse, and which she uses to pad the temperatures to impress her relatives who live downstate. Still doesn't mean it's safe to snowmobile across the canal— look at the temp. pattern of recent weeks to get a better feeling for it, or, better, don't even try it at all. Timothy has a snowmobile and loves to ride across the ice on days like this against Harriet's sisterly suggestion—and he should listen, considering all that's happened. But he's dumb and young. So cold it's like you're invincible, too stiff and wrapped-up to break. Memory of Liz crouched down with that armless boy in the cold, she so kind and he so strange and quiet.

-38 — how cold it gets routinely in places like Fargo and smaller towns in North Dakota; unbelievable how they live, though maybe that's where she should go for purgatory, as a step toward becoming invisible in the constant chill, the car-glass crack, and forget Liz and auto accidents and the numbers permanently marked on the body. You have to put cardboard up in the grates of your car to keep the engine block from freezing. Special windshield washer fluid. Extreme antifreeze and oil. Plug your truck into the outlet at night to have even a chance at starting up again come morning.

-40 — all time record low in Northern Florida, state featured on the last postcard received from Liz—a running joke between the two of them, the love of stupid postcards: "Wish you were here in Sunny Florida/Georgia/Las Vegas/Death Valley where the World's Biggest Pecan/Pelican/Crucifix/Twine Ball is, Yours Forever, Liz." Was this meant as final words? Or was this her intention—to keep up the correspondence even after she had gone?

-44 — all-time record low natural temperature in Northern Michigan. All-time record number of people dying that year, but not H. and Liz and not her stalker, all invincible, still young. Memory of the names listed in the paper. Memory of Liz and her near-admiring *At least that's one way out* and the silence reverberating after. Memory of not understanding and going home alone, being swallowed in the snow.

-268 — big jump now, approaching the big atomic, scientific death, this is as close as she knows we have ever come to the big absolute, and this was only in very rigidly controlled conditions—what those are, she doesn't know.

-271 — does even light begin to slow, approximating lines then dashes like in the movies? Will her responsibility then begin to fade? She must admit that she's attracted to this clarity, this permanent anesthesia.

-273 — which means absolute zero in Kelvin, she remembers, maybe wrong, from school, where she would sit in Chemistry or whatever class it was behind her Liz. Always facing the neck's back, the fine hairs and salt traces. Harriet usually in pursuit, in clouds of hairspray or exhaust. Maybe it's Celsius, the scale she wishes they'd use—so simple—but it would take some getting used to. Plus there's a certain panache to using the English measures—a way of thinking that is nearly obsolete but that we cling onto with our sad hands and frozen hairs on end.

-273 — everything stops when it gets this cold, even the atoms stop their baby steps and spinning. Even Liz gone ghost and in the paper. Even Liz in action with her crowd of boys who were not all boys anymore. Even Liz with that one boy, her stalker friend who thought he knew that he and Liz were more than friends, that sad and stupid kid, who gave Harriet (after Liz was gone and gone and gone) half a lock of Liz's hair as a memento because (he said) she had loved her too. Even when he had refused to clarify his pronoun ambiguity and left her standing there. Even Liz submerged in the icy water, or buried in the icy ground, even the dead tributaries of Harriet's family, her lonely body, and her brother on his way back from school on his snowmobile, and the atoms within him. Even the sound waves carrying their essential information: messages from Liz suspended somewhere in the air or memory, her last *Don't go, it's early yet*, her last *Turn it up*, her last *I love this song*. This is cold enough to stop the speed of thought, of any kind of life or useful motion. Maybe this is just impossible, so theory-cold. Even her overtime waking daydreams stop when she's worked so many hours she can't see the road in front of her but keeps it all going out of force of habit and knowledge of her section of road, out of thoughts of spring, returning, which she knows it will, with its reassuring thaw and the birth of the million bugs. She will spend more time with her road this year and minister to it like a body, heavy, soft. She will treat it like a monument. She knows some guys who piss on theirs like dogs.

Dream Obits
for Liz

Elizabeth, eighteen years old, died yesterday when her car went through the ice.

Elizabeth, Journey fan, good and experimental kisser, left the world with the radio on, which is something, we suppose.

Elizabeth left behind no one worth mentioning. Viewing and visitation, an abbreviation for our love and dot dot dot.

Elizabeth, eighteen, now gone numb, unsung, and eh.

Elizabeth, eighteen, from Eagle River or Agate Beach. Someplace with shine, not Misery Bay or the cold lake with the dredge.

Elizabeth, eighteen, whom you could never be sure of.

Elizabeth, eighteen, clammy hands, a renunciation, an echo from a mix tape in a car.

Elizabeth went through like a lark would go through stained glass or anything like that.

Elizabeth went through of her own volition, maybe.

Elizabeth whose keys weren't found in the ignition, weren't found at all.

Elizabeth not made like the rest of us.

Elizabeth not made for this.

Elizabeth made-up and unmade.

Elizabeth the former burnout, who kept cigarettes romantic in her bra.

Elizabeth whose name was cut into the paint on bathroom doors.

Elizabeth whose curls of smoke echoed her passing through the halls, her hand-print fading on a locker.

Elizabeth cast in the dullest role.

Elizabeth, unreprised in future sequels.

Elizabeth found in scraps.

Elizabeth, eighteen, not the first to leave our class for ice and foreign lands, but the first one I miss like this.

Elizabeth a scrap of longitude and tongue.

Elizabeth, a sort-of Icarus, inverted.

Elizabeth gone myth.

Elizabeth: dyed roots and bottlecap.

Elizabeth now made of ash.

Elizabeth my new Cousteau.

Elizabeth my subterranean.

Elizabeth the only answer to this equation.

Elizabeth: causal, casual, casualty.

Elizabeth, suddenly astonished at her predicament.

Elizabeth cast in glass.

Elizabeth my term my definition.

Elizabeth my itch and inch and ink.

Elizabeth my etc.

Elizabeth just etc.

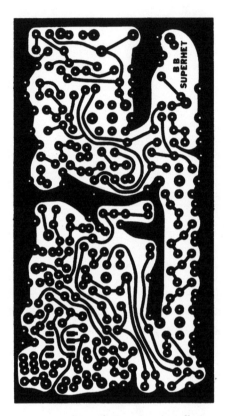

———— *Dear, distance is a constellation,*
dead light from distant stars

A Huge,
Old Radio

Christer waits his turn, shirtless, in the dark. He hears his friends' voices tossing back and forth in the quiet, wet air up ahead, punctuated by spurts of canned music and talk coming from behind, open car windows a hundred feet back on M-26 through Baraga, through L'Anse, by the Reservation. They're here to jump off the rushing spout of Canyon Falls into the pool below. An early winter rite. A flashlight glances across the rocky pathway and disappears. A brief "Cannonball!" and a second of silence, then a muffled two-tone splash—*ba-whoosh*—somewhere up ahead.

It's October. The first snowfall hit last night and was gone by morning, burned off by a warm late fall sun—probably the last day before real, sticking snow. The snow here comes and goes, piles up and gets burned off, until it settles in for six months, collecting dirt, salt, and urine, blackening on the sides of roads and plowed driveways.

The cars parked in the short two-rut road off the highway are in disrepair. Jelly's Aerostar with the driver's side mirror bashed off, hanging by a black cord. Crisco's old key-scratched blue Ford Fairlane running only through the grace of God he says, kept with a King James Bible and a Virgin Mary figurine in the cracked dashboard recess. People feel up the Virgin Mary and tear out the pages in the Bible when they ride with him. Because the car's metal body is so rusted out from road salt and extended winter, you can see space in the walls and the floor. There's a huge hole in the back of the roof in which rain collects, spawning bugs and mosquitoes that bite backs and necks.

Christer has taken his dad's climate-controlled company car without permission, a Lincoln Mark VIII with speakers and working sound. This is the only still-whole car in the group, but no one will ride with him—he doesn't have a full license yet. Only half the group likes him. He's a week shy of sixteen.

Throwing a quick hopeful glance over his shoulder, he can't make out the vehicles hidden in the black air. It's so dark, he can smell boys' bodies clearly up ahead but can't see. No one's speaking. The line is halted. Thin Rupert must be up ahead, teetering on the edge, his breath stuck, his fingers grasping in his pockets for his inhaler. "Hey guys?"

"Jump, you fuck!"

Chuckles echo from someone else up ahead.

"Who's that up there?"

"Listen—"

Tony is telling the Goat Boy story again.

Everyone knows the story; everyone listens. Laughter breaks out when he gets to *The Cross! The Cross!* part. It's not as funny, though, this time. Christer can hear wet, asthmatic hacking from below. Like something from a movie or a book. Like emphysema and the breathing machines his grandfather had in the last month of his life. The story doesn't work as well in this place, this particular dark. It feels like they're in something's mouth.

The words get lost in the wet air, among the birch trees that populate these woods like huge white vertical bars. Tony's mom died last year. Nobody talks about it. The image of her offering fruit salad in a big red bowl to everyone at Halloween, face wide in a cherry-lipsticked smile, keeps coming back to Christer, breaking down his laugh, making it mechanical, dysfunctional, strange.

And then there's Carrie. And Crisco left behind, angry as the storms that rage through Michigan in winter.

He feels stupid.

Tiny pinpricks of cold all over his neck and back. It must be snowing again. The cold makes his skin feel hot. *Move ahead.*

He hears a half-caught breath and reaches out ahead of him to touch Tony's skin, but finds nothing, feels the air swirling. A splash down below.

"Yeah, that shit." Rupert's voice comes up reinforced from below.

A dash of laughter cut off in the middle. A smell like old dirt under a house, moving, filled with pill bugs and sticky worms.

"Ya fucking shitball."

Tiny hairs poke out, erect, from his legs.

"God it—"

He can feel the edge falling away, disintegrating under his toes. The air from below moves against his chest, melting the snow before it hits his body, so he's crowned with hundreds of tiny drops. From below it might look bright and gleaming, like sweat when the flashlight moves across. He thinks he might look like Jesus. He's the last one in line.

"Get your ass . . ." The flashlight vanishes.

It's different up here against the edge. Everything below is hidden in the swirling, gently snowing darkness. Christer can hear their broken muttering coming up from below. For an instant, he thinks the world might be a huge, old radio, alive and electric with voice and squeal, the crossover of stations bleeding into one another. Like the kind Tony has in his living room, with a big luminescent dial that clicks when you turn it, and a knotty wood cabinet—the signal coming in clear then breaking up into a static hush, repeating.

"Shouldn't . . . cold . . ."

He's steaming now. Like pasta in a colander. Or a breast fresh from the bath seen through the old keyhole in a door. The air around the freshly dead.

The flashlight comes up against him again, illuminating the air around his thin wet chest. Smoking, burning off. He wonders how he looks, who he is right now. An overcooked potato, he inhales, raises his arms, lets the pits breathe. A shiver. Strobe effect. Sublime. He thinks about his mom, and Tony's mom, and Carrie, tries to summon a sharp clear image of all three at one time but can't hold it. He starts to breathe out, leans forward, and lets himself go—drops like a spinning cat's-eye marble in a deep, deep well—into the cooling black air. He falls. Dark. Free in this moment. Melting. The stars disintegrating in the sky. The radio waves through and through him. The air below warming with his passage, moving up. Slices of Bon Jovi. Everything steam and motion. Filter. A vector. Depth and car alarm. Snow and snow and snow.

Isle Royale

There's a joke that kids tell around here that goes like this: *What happened to the* Ranger? / *It sunk.* / *What happened to the* Ranger II? / *It sunk.* / *What'll happen to the* Ranger III? / *It's gonna sink.*

I never said it was a funny joke. I don't know why it's even a joke. I don't know how it got its jokehood. But kids around here say it. We used to laugh our asses off at it. Maybe we were all cracked out, or maybe we're assholes. I don't know.

Tony and me'd go down to where the *Ranger III* was moored when it wasn't making trips out to Isle Royale, the eye in the wolf's head on the map that's Lake Superior. The eye is the island, with its hiking trails and campgrounds and its pines and wolves and moose. People take the boat out there every year. That or else they take a seaplane. I never went. Neither'd Tony.

We'd go down to the docks, though, me and him, on some nights before he left for Michigan State ten hours away in Lansing, and we'd throw eggs off the docks, throw them on the huge rusted hull that makes up the big boat. We'd come with a couple dozen and keep throwing—

pong! pong! pong!—until somebody'd come and yell at us, then we'd take off and laugh. Sometimes nobody even noticed and we'd just get finished and leave the egg cartons on the concrete.

The boat is huge and blue. I'm here alone tonight, with eggs but just watching. A few years ago the seniors, super-seniors, and hangers-on used to sneak up on the *Ranger III* in the nights and spray-paint stupid shit on the sides about who loves who and who sucks ass but nobody does that anymore. I don't know why. It's just dumb now.

When I was growing up we'd always see *Jesse + Tammy '84* or *Bulldogs Suck* sprayed on the side of the boat when it slid slowly through the canal on its way out there. They'd blow the sea-horn so they'd raise the bridge and stop the traffic, then me and my friends would sit on the side of the road and watch it slowly skate through the gap. Two more blasts on the horn and the bridge would start to lower back down.

There were girls I knew who went out to Isle Royale with guys for the weekend. They'd grin about it all week long. I never got to go, see. Tony and me used to make plans to invite girls we knew out there with us or maybe we'd say fuck all that and go ourselves. Just spontaneous and shit. We'd bring some matches and a knife and maybe a couple garbage bags for a tarp that we could sleep under. I only went camping a couple of times and it pretty much sucked. However, there are cool things: dried fir trees—yellow, orange, and brown—sound like firecrackers when you throw them in a fire. They flare up and bristle into the night.

Tony's a frickin' genius. He made the move downstate last year, working on his engineering degree. Most of us prefer to stay and go to Tech. Others stay and go directly to the bars. But Tony made the move out, downstate.

The night before he moved down, we egged Mr. Lechman's place. He's the old Geometry teacher with a lisp. Always fun to get a rise out of him, but Tony had to leave early in the morning and the car still wasn't packed, so we didn't waste too much time before we got it done. Covered the garage door, almost took out a window even though we weren't aiming at it. Don't know if he was even home, the fucker.

There's not many ways out of here. Two hours in your dad's car will get you to the state line, into Wisconsin. I tried that once. I made the border in good time—saw the sign and everything—but drove on and it kept bringing me back in Michigan. *Welcome to Michigan. Welcome to Wisconsin. Welcome to Michigan.*

It wasn't much different for the few minutes I was in Wisconsin, though. It was pretty much the same. Drunks trolling the snowy streets. Bars outnumber churches. They have strip clubs there, though, if that's your thing. And it's an hour back of us. Eastern Time becomes Central Time, and back again. You lose an hour, then gain one, and back, and you don't know what time it is really, don't know which clock to trust.

You can take a car east and six hours and hit Canada. Tried that way, too. Tony and me were visiting his grandparents and taking out his grandma's safe because she said she didn't need it anymore, and we had it in the back of his rusted-ass Aerostar and we took it out and decided since we were bored that we'd go from Sault Ste. Marie, Michigan, to Sault Ste. Marie, Canada. There's a long bridge. About five clean minutes over the lake to get there. And we got there and got stopped in Customs. We had the safe in the back and so they separated us and asked us where we were from, what our license plate number was, what was in the safe. It scared me. The safe was locked. We didn't know the combination. There could've been anything inside.

They sent us back to the States. Which was probably the best that could've happened, considering they were prepared to call somebody to crack open the safe. Maybe Tony called his grandparents or something and they got us out of it. I don't know.

Nobody's out tonight. Festival Foods cashiers don't even look at me funny anymore when I come in at one or two a.m. and buy a couple dozen eggs, a ski mask, and some smokes. I only brought one styrofoam carton of the Jilbert's Dairy eggs this time. I light up. The air's cool. My fingers trace the outline of the carton, its indentations and weight.

The other way is by plane. They don't come much through Houghton, but every other day the Mesaba propeller planes come through and touch down for minutes. Pick up a few folks, drop a few off. Before she left for the cancer ward and then the crematorium, my mom was in one of those and the engine cut out and it dropped 4000 feet before regaining control. They made an emergency landing in Grand Rapids. She took the bus back up. I'm not never going that way.

Every year, somebody takes the easy way and goes through the ice on a snowmobile. Sometimes it's a few kids a year. Idiots. Of course, sometimes somebody makes it up to speed and spits across the water and comes back on ice, unscathed. I wonder if you try it again.

Somebody set the record last year for going twelve miles over open water when he left the ice behind him on Lake Superior. He must've been going pretty damn fast. You gotta be going fast on one of those to hold yourself up over water. And if you go down, you're gonna freeze. Nobody's there to save your ass.

But every year somebody tries to snowmobile across the canal. Nobody learns shit, they think the dead just went about it all wrong. About January, they go for it again. The president of Michigan Tech's son drowned that way, he went through the ice and made the paper, like the others.

I throw a couple eggs at the side of the boat and they hit and resonate. It's like a song.

I heard the ice just gave out on him and he went through. The son of the school president. And all the others.

In the winter sometimes the icebreakers come through to clear the path for iron ore boats or the *Ranger III* on its way out to Isle Royale for the unusual trip, the winter campers I guess. The ice behind it gets cut in chunks and it bobs up and down in the cold cold water. In a couple hours it seals back up and it's safe to go out there again. The seam's still there though it's frozen.

But that kid, he went out on a snappy clean January day when it was sub-zero and clear. Clear days are the coldest, you understand. He went out, maybe he was drunk or maybe he was just dumb. There wasn't no excuse, no good reason for it. The *Ranger* was moored in its dock, not enough kids to give it reason to make a run. No icebreakers had been through in weeks. The ice should've been thick as an arm or two, but you never know. That's what somebody thinks every year.

You go out drunk or not drunk, and contrary to what the hell you expected, you hear a sharp snap, maybe it's the sound of a high ping, a shift, a fault opening up, maybe it's nothing you hear at all but something you feel, and at a good speed, too, you're going maybe forty or sixty miles an hour and at that speed, you can't do nothing, can't recover from something like that.

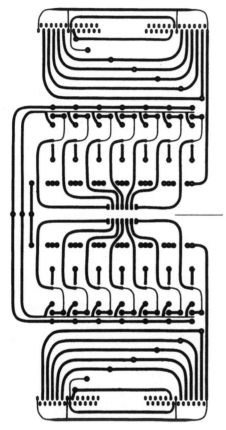

Dear, distance is the center of the world, unbearable like magna, untouchable like gas

Residue

1 / Getting Rid of the Body

Christer parts the tall grass with his hands as he makes his way back through the field. The ground is slick with July rain and dark below the gold stalks of grass. He wades through the thick, sharp stuff, accumulating tiny cuts on his forearms until the Plymouth rises up fat and blue out of nowhere. Looking carefully at the door to the car, he sees that it is jammed shut, bent in, the handle lying hopelessly on the ground. When he picks it up and holds it close to his face, he can see rust spots fragmenting the metal into shapes of tiny, five-fingered stars. He drops it back on the ground, where it settles into its impression in the earth.

He kicks the door and it squeals open. A stack of twenty or so magazines slides out onto the wet grass. He looks closer. They have rotted out from the center and spots of mold cover them all.

Christer looks at the magazines. They are pornos, sure enough. He can see skin white with mold and rotted through; breasts falling apart at the sides and spilling splashes of garish color through from the pages below; pubic hair breaking off and merging with other patches of pubic hair. These are bodies in the process of decomposing and expanding toward a mass of posed, rotting limbs—the waiting room in a crematorium for mannequins.

His older brother drowned while snowmobiling across the canal in the middle of January. Though everyone knew the newspaper details, that fat Bernard had gone through a patch of thin ice and sunk to the bottom, Christer has always wanted to know the mechanics of the sinking: Did the ice slowly crack and buckle, then finally give way, or was it quick—his big body dumped without warning? Was he thrown or did he ride it all the way down, his fingers clutching the molded rubber grips of his Polaris Indy Classic, the ridges of his knuckles slowly sinking from flesh pink to white?

He has the newspaper article in his room, sealed in a Ziploc bag. He spent almost every night for a year looking at the newsprint close-up through a magnifying glass, trying to break down the words into the everyday truth of his brother's absence buried in the weave and grain of the paper.

When he first heard, he walked out with no jacket to what he thought was the exact spot of his brother's descent. He remembers looking down at the smooth, newly clotted ice. In his mind, he can see the outline of the hole shining like a dull, wet star—pointed with five chubby cracks reaching out, and then finally vanishing, filled in by something darker, new.

Pastor Sam, who tried to talk to Christer after Bernard's death, had said that miracles could sometimes happen, that a human body could sometimes be revived thirty minutes after it stops breathing if the water was cold enough. Christer didn't know what to say, exactly, to that.

They recovered the machine—it was illegal to leave it down there because of pollution. Someone went through the ice every year on a snowmobile, and Christer could imagine the leftover, accumulating snow-mobiles, tossing with the current, slowly gathering in metallic, junky clots.

Bernard's snowmobile is still in the garage, covered with a fraying blue plastic tarp that blows off easily. Christer had tied it down with double overhand knots, but it had come loose one windy January day when someone had left the side door cracked open—you had to pull it shut and listen for the click, especially in the winter, when the metal contracted. The tarp had blown off in a gust of wind when his mom had come in to get chicken breasts out of the deep freeze. She has said that she cried out, dropping her knees hard to the cold concrete, bruising them purple. Christer imagines his mother there in the garage, snow whirling fast in tight circles around her and the snowmobile, making it look as if they are both resting on thin, black ice.

When his mom and dad decided to have Bernard cremated, they left Christer at home. He had overheard them talking about it beforehand, and looked up the crematorium in the Yellow Pages. There was only one, so he decided to walk. When he finally got there, though, it didn't look at all as he expected: The driveway was plowed and graded down to sheer ice, and there was a silver mailbox planted like a stiff marigold at its end. A fence was mostly buried in snow, and the building itself was like a house, small and white with green trim. The windows were blocked up with black or dark green curtains, so he couldn't see inside; two huge chimneys towered up into the sky like circular, severed legs.

Christer couldn't bring himself to go in, so he wandered around outside, thinking of Bernard and Pastor Sam, making snow angels then disliking their shape, obscuring them with his feet. He imagined his brother's body being slowly fed into the flames while his parents watched. It was a Thursday. He took the mail and read it. There were bills (gas, electric, phone) and promotional fliers from Wal-Mart. They were beginning their seasonal sale.

Christer considers the pile of magazines collected at his feet, made up mostly of old copies of *Swank* and *Penthouse*, smelling like hospitals and bread. He wrinkles his nose and glances around him: peeling white birches, bark strips hanging down like striped, angry snakes. He turns his attention back to the magazines, and stands for a second, indecisive. He scratches one of the scabbed-over cuts on his forearm, then slowly licks the inside of his wrist, following the vein up into the palm with his tongue. Disentangling himself from the paper, he steps back, then watches the pile collapse in where his feet have just been, loose and white in the sneakers—as if he had never been there, as if his presence had nothing to do with either discovery or decay.

He closes his eyes and then opens them slowly, teaching himself as Pastor Sam has said he must do every day to remember his brother's form.

Feeling suddenly unsteady, he sits down abruptly into the sloppy grass. His corduroys will be stained, he knows. He thinks he feels a wall of scratched Plexiglas just in front of him. His cheek presses cold against it; his mouth opens and closes on hard absence. He can see through it, but the tiny scratches and indents on the glass itself draw his attention away from what's on the other side, so much so that it is entirely eclipsed from his vision and the glass becomes completely opaque. When he closes and reopens his eyes, it is gone. Things like this often occur in the normal day-to-day functioning of his life, momentary hallucinations, flashbacks almost, except that there is nothing to flashback to. He thinks that maybe there are cracks in the world that open up for a moment, and then drop back into place like a curtain. The curtain is black and heavy, smelling of dust and paper.

Christer remembers when he saw his brother masturbating with a copy of *Hustler*. He watches Bernard shut the bedroom door and can hear it lock from the inside, and wonders why he would bother to lock it. In a sort of trance, he watches himself slowly turn the handle on the screen door and step outside to look in through the slatted blinds of Bernard's window. He remembers his brother as a rolled whale on top of a flat, yellow pillow, moving his fist under his belly in quiet circular motions, eyes fixed on the shiny pages inches in front of his face. He moves back, and watches himself watch his brother through the window. The slats in the blinds cut Bernard into twenty-two distinct layers of memory and file him away.

He moves around the car in a slow orbit. Bernard found this spot originally the summer before he died and brought his friend, Bone, and his brother here to show it off. Christer had watched as Bone and Bernard swung the rubber-handled hammer in repeated arcs at the windshield, giggling loudly and splitting the glass into hundreds of translucent blue squares. Christer has returned here once after Bernard's death, then again after Pastor Sam's stroke, and has used the hammer to break the rear window and the glass along the passenger side, leaving the same arcs of motion behind him. The glass broke cleanly that time, shattering on the vinyl backseat and the ground. When he looked down, he could see himself reflected separately in each piece.

Here again, Christer can feel the residue of the hammer-motion somehow still present in the air around him. It resonates slowly and recycles, refusing to dissipate into the remaining world. Though he tries to remember the car as he first saw it, glass clean and unbroken, he cannot. The only intact parts of the car are the two headlights, which look entirely new and out of place. If he could somehow turn on the car, fit an old, clumsy key into the ignition, generate an electrical current, then Christer is sure they would shine and illuminate whatever they faced.

It's still daylight, and he looks at his arm, covered with tiny droplets of sweat, in each of which he is sure that, if he looks closely enough, he will see a slightly different replica of the world around him. He licks the underside of his wrist again to remind himself of how it feels—the vein a thin blue ridge pulsing slowly under the skin. He crawls closer into the pile, surrounding himself with the magazines like a castle wall, and begins to slowly flip through the pages.

Christer used to peep in windows on Sunday nights. He would slip out the back screen door, taking care not to let it bang shut, and he would track around the neighborhood, looking for lighted rooms and open curtains. He liked to see what people were cooking for dinner, whether they prayed before eating, how they moved when they were alone. Once, there was an entire family sitting cross-legged on the floor, watching a test pattern on television. As he watched, it changed to snow. In his memory, the screen is reflected, minimized and distorted, in each set of eyes. There is a small angel statuette perched on the window. Christer moves it a few inches to the right and notices the ring it leaves behind in the dust.

He particularly liked watching elderly people with very young children. They held them more softly, watched them more carefully, seemed to see their lives reflected in their eyes. On slow Sunday nights, Mrs. Hambley would hold her grandson in her arms, rocking very slowly, just watching. Christer could feel a transference taking place.

o

In the years since his brother's death, Christer has collected Christmas trees. Just after the holiday, when people put their trees out on the street to be collected by the garbage men, he drags them off over his shoulder if they aren't too large, or tows them away, balanced on his wagon, pine needles dropping off behind him. He has a particular spot in the woods where he brings and suspends them, tied up by heavy twine, in oak trees. There is one old oak in the forest where sixteen desiccated pine trees dangle from its upper branches. He uses a makeshift pulley system to haul them up, and ties them in bowlines around the thick branches, close in to the trunk. These knots hold a special place in Christer's heart. They won't ever come loose, he has tied them so tightly—the trees will hang forever, until the oak trunk snaps under the weight of frozen water or whirling snow, or is blown apart by lightning.

He likes to stand under the oak sometimes, looking up at the trees— they're mostly bare now, but once men and women, families, brothers had clustered around each of them, opening wrapped presents, gazing at blinking white or colored lights. He can see from below that there are still a few traces of tinsel that people have left behind. This always makes him think of Christmas Eve in his church: baskets of steaming, foil-wrapped food; huge, hanging coats on silver hooks; long chains of paper rings; heavy, shaking bags of glue and glitter.

The trunks swing back and forth, and creak quietly in the wind. He hears one tiny silver berry bell tinkling, buried forgotten and deep.

He has read that, farther south, people drag their Christmas trees to the lake where it hasn't yet frozen over, and slide them quietly into the water. Christer watches this happen over and over in his mind until the sequence of images leave footprints in his memory and dull red tracks on his retinas, so that he can see the outlines of their motion whenever he closes his eyes. Now in his dreams he watches the trees, slick with cold, pile up in the basin at the bottom of the lake. The needles drop off in clumps like hair, and the bark slowly peels off and floats to the surface, leaving behind piles of gleaming white, interlocking skeletons of bone.

But now he sits, looking through pages of dead and rotting paper. Nakedness is a belly on a pillow, a face submarining in icy water, a body slowly reduced to ashes. Christer watches the pages go by, and regards his fingers oddly as they turn over each new leaf, revealing more and more broken, decomposing flesh. He wills his fingers to stop their progress, and he puts down the magazines. He comes to his feet with a start.

A drop of rain slaps fatly in the direct center of his forehead. He looks up, waiting, but nothing comes. Just dry, white sky. There is a muted booming sound, and he watches as a single firework explodes, flowering out in flashing, golden petals. When the petals and the blast have faded out of the sky, they are followed by a second, which illuminates the smoke trails of the first with its bright explosion as everything falls quietly to earth.

2 / Kissing Bernard

Christer remembers being trapped, against the ridged brown carpet in the family room, under his brother's weight. He is on his back, trying to scream, but the noise from the three-speed fan swallows up his sounds with its open, humming mouth. Bernard is laughing and reaching to hike his shirt up over his huge belly.

"You're gonna kiss it."

Christer shakes his head and bites hard into the thumb-knuckle on his brother's hand. Bernard shakes the meaty paw free and slams it into Christer's cheek, leaving it warm and shocked.

"Kiss my tummy."

Christer is quiet now, underwater—not moving, only rasping. "I can't breathe."

"Kiss it and I'll let you up."

Christer lifts his head slightly and watches as the image of Bernard begins to blur and double, his two eyes merging into one huge blinking eye, his mouth becoming a thin strip of teeth and heavy, wet tongue, his big skin darkening. In this moment, Christer knows he hates his brother, then things begin to fade and he is suddenly aware of his hands opening and closing swiftly, reaching, then a strange wetness in his crotch, then nothing at all as his head drops back, burying itself into the surface of the ground.

3 / A Waiting Room

Christer remembers when he was nine and Pastor Sam had a stroke. He watches himself hold his mother's hand as they visit the hospital, a place with curtains shrouding bodies and vast murals of white. He pauses his memory at the frame which holds a close-up of his fingers twined into his mother's, like roots of trees that grow close together and become indistinguishable. He remembers smelling bread, and his mother telling him no one is baking. He remembers the floor, not quite flat, but gently hilled along the edges, so a red-and-white top or a cat's-eye marble would spin or roll to the exact center and stay there until kicked or crushed.

Christer wants to ask him about Bernard, but his mother says that Pastor Sam can't respond, though he can understand everything they say. He is not sure who his mother is talking to. Pastor Sam's head rests on a flat white pillow, and his fingers move in small circles when he tries to speak. His breathing stutters with each syllable, but he can't seem to produce any real sound. Pastor Sam can blink his left eye but not his right. The right eye is closed and quivers lightly but never opens more than halfway or closes completely. He remembers his mother making him kneel by the bedside and recite the Lord's prayer, with "Debts" for Pastor Sam, not "Trespasses" like he was taught. On his knees against the bed, Christer looks up at Pastor Sam's fingers, the knuckles big and cracking out of the skin, whirling and leaving halos behind in the air, and it is exactly now that he knows he is dying.

He imagines standing on a vinyl chair and watching Pastor Sam from above, watching a wet spot on his stomach expand. Christer has now begun to doubt the actual existence of this spot, but his memory shows it plain and anatomical: red soaking through just above the belly button and slowly permeating the sheet, spreading outward in a circle until it drips off the edge, and Christer stops the memory there: the droplet of blood in sudden transition from sheet to floor. He now doubts the fidelity of this memory because he later read in an encyclopedia with a heavy cover that strokes don't cause bleeding in the abdominal area. He starts his memory again: the droplet of blood resumes its fall and hits the floor, and that's when his mother says something about the indivisibility of God, and Pastor Sam moves his arm, and Christer falls to the floor and watches the ceiling rotate instead of the fan.

4 / Boundaries and the Newly Deceased

Christer's walking with Pastor Sam through a long and straight row of evergreens. Pastor Sam says they must've been planted like that, in straight lines and parallel rows, because nature doesn't do that by itself.

Christer looks up—there are gaps through which the sun filters down in spots to the ground. Neither of them is talking about Bernard, but it hangs in the air. It's a month after the drowning.

"The air's cold, but these are my favorite woods," says Pastor Sam. Christer's freckles are sharp against the glistening white snow. "Want to know why?"

"Yeah, I guess," says Christer, the gap in his teeth showing.

"Because it's just so quiet here—it's quieter than just quiet. I mean, if there were no air and no sound, it would be quiet, but here it's different. Here it's actively quiet."

Christer doesn't understand and says so.

"It's like a blanket. It covers everything. Stop for a second—." They do. Everything ceases and the quiet widens. Sam lets it go. "Can you hear that?"

"Yeah."

"You know what I mean?"

"Yeah, I think I get it."

Christer thinks to himself as Pastor Sam lets the silence stretch again. It's like the white space in a frame. It's like milk in a bottle. Bounded. It has to be maintained to keep its shape.

Pastor Sam lets the silence drop and points. "See that wasp's nest in the crook of that V-shape up there?"

"Yeah, I think so." It looks like a tiny paper ball hanging from the underside of a limb, like the fat flap from his brother's arm.

"You almost never see wasps' nests in trees. And never in pine trees."

"Really? Why not?"

"I don't know, but it doesn't happen that way." Sam wants to say something here, wants to get Christer talking. He needs to get it out; like gas, it's flammable, a push that could become a burst, or a fire. "Do you miss your brother?"

There's just a space now, bounded by the end of the question and the expected response. It's a dip. Christer doesn't know what to say. He's not sure. "I'm sorry it all happened like that. That's all I know."

"I understand." Pastor Sam touches Christer's elbow lightly in what he hopes is a reassuring way. Something's buried, needs to come up.

5 / Digging up Treasure

Christer is looking at the map, searching for a bluff. He is holding two washed-out ice-cream buckets in his right hand as his feet slide over the mossy path he knows will lead him to the two spruce trees which will, in turn, lead him to where Bernard's ashes are buried. He turns his head to the ground to see trillium and bloodroot passing by beneath him, leaving lines of white in his mind, to let his feet and hands lead him to where his head will not.

They do. He is past the spruces and is facing the bluff before Christer can lift his head again. There is a massive, overhanging Douglas fir, its roots covered with browning moss. The earth has eroded almost halfway beneath it, but it refuses to fall. It has been three years since he stole his brother's ashes from the mantelpiece in the family room, replacing them with a combination of normal wood ash, ceramic dust, and fine sand, and brought them out here in a coffee can. It has been three years of hanging Christmas trees since he buried his brother in the clay. Christer puts down the empty buckets and blinks his eyes once before going to his knees to dig up the coffee can which contains the remains of Bernard. His knuckles remember, and they direct the fingers to scrape away the inches of loose sand before they reach the wet, sloppy clay. He has brought a small knife with him to help him cut it out, but it is slow going. He cuts and peels the wet stuff off in layers. They get darker as he goes down. He piles them in heavy sheets next to the hole.

Christer nearly cuts himself when he hits the sheet of slate marking the spot, the blade deflecting off and just missing his other hand. He pries it up and touches his fingers quietly to the lid of the can below. He pushes it to see if it will move, but it won't. He thinks that maybe Bernard is not only inside the can, but maybe part of him has seeped out into the surrounding clay. He cuts out the clay and collects it in the two buckets, then uses both hands to pull out the coffee can. It pops free and Christer falls back with the can in his lap, his arms around it in an unintentional hug. He looks at it for a moment, then places it down on the ground; then he leans back into the pile of fresh, wet clay, mashes his head and back into it, sliding his arms over the earth, leaving a sort of clay angel behind him.

He lies there, losing the warmth and color of his skin.

After a minute, he stands and picks up the two buckets of clay, along with the coffee can, and begins to walk back, leaving behind the hole and the angel, gaping together in the earth.

6 / Lying Under the Belly of the World

Sitting back, Christer looks up at his creation. It is a globe of shiny paper, car glass, and ashes wet with gasoline from home, cemented together with clay, saliva, and rubber cement. It is two feet in diameter, and hangs from a blue spruce tree, suspended with heavy twine six-and-a-half feet off the ground, tied with a simple square knot. He has disassembled the stack of pornos and balled some up, then wrapped others around, creating a spherical collage of nipples and belly buttons, freckles, noses, and patches of hair. He has pulled the broken, rubber-backed sheets of car glass out of the Plymouth and spread them over the ball like a blanket. He has covered the whole thing in clay, then taken some of the remaining pages of text from the magazines and wadded them up into continental shapes, until all that was left were the decaying covers, and so Christer has built an exact replica of the world.

He remembers reading how Odysseus escaped the Cyclops by strapping himself and his comrades under the bellies of sheep, so he lies down on the ground, in the slippery grass, below the porno and car glass globe, and watches the blades of grass magnify themselves like the pores of the torn models above him, expanding and beginning to suck him in, breasts waving, and suddenly he cannot breathe under the weight of the motion blazing like fireflies on slow film in the air around him; and as he has clipped out the newspaper article about his brother going through the ice and has held it under the magnifying glass for so long that the ink letters pixellate and blur out until he can't see his brother's face anymore or anything else, he then moves the magnifying glass back so that the light closes from a wonderful ring to a tiny point in the middle of the word "memorial" and sets the whole thing on fire.

The Organization
and Formation of Blizzards
as Seen by Satellites: A–M

As if this onrush of wind and sleet and auto accident could easily be studied. As if it could be tracked by screens by light on screens and telemetric shadow from above. As if we can understand it. As if we can predict it. Because prediction is the goal—a sad runner-up to prevention. Because at least we can have warning. Because we can tell or know to go inside. Because it offers subjects for discussion. Because the big one in 1979 brought down the barn and topped the record book. Because we can measure something means we can identify and track it. Can this storm be discrete? Can we get to your aunt's in time? Can we analyze its conceptual model to be more accurately predictive in the future? Can you handle all the ice sheeting on the roads? Can we shovel it all off or melt it all away? Did your mother avoid disaster? Did she get inside in time, or is she out in it, her tongue protruding hot and wet and letting snowflakes hurl themselves into her jaw? Did she get the neighbor boy to shovel off her roof last week or should she expect ice to come down from above? Exothermic reactions in blizzards, of fronts colliding with each other, sometimes resulting in lightning. Expect the worst. Expect to have to go out in it. Expect that you can't stay inside forever. Ex-wife potential—a depressing thought and one unfair to her since the rift was not her fault but yours. Forecasting accuracy. Forecasting for aviation with colored graphics. Forecasting the movement of fronts that bring freezing rain down upon us like a punishment from God. God's anger sheets everything in glass and brittleness, like information and the state of your marriage. How shoveling in the winter glare and falling is pleasure-labor, a way of making measurable progress. If all this freezing rain is justified retribution, why does it leave such loveliness behind—everything quiet and tinkling in the remaining winds? If all this is preamble to apocalypse, that explains the creaking limbs, the ice age rehearsal. If all this global warming is coming to an end, should we expect less snow or more next year? If the storms move past us in through the night, will schools open up tomorrow, or will the gusting and the winds be strong enough to keep the kids still home and hot with chocolate and repetitious games of Connect Four. Just let it pass to keep them home. Just let the temperature crest into the teens tomorrow morning so we can stay home from work and enjoy ourselves. Just let us get on skis and go cross-country, rifles strapped across our backs in case of ambush or biathlon. Keep us warm and safe indoors, double-glass storm windows with extra insulation and the plastic wrap stretched tight across it. Keep us up late enough to put the kids to bed and watch the snow accumulate as we predict how much will fall tonight. Keep us up so we can work on our marriage. Keep us off our feet to let the recently-broken bones knit and stitch themselves together while we sleep. LAPS precipitation graphic, created from radar reflectivity and 3-D temperature, downloaded from the Internet for use in a later report. Major snowstorms we have known. Major snowstorms we have weathered. Major snowstorms classified as blizzards due to velocity of wind. Major U.S. catastrophes, 1950-1994, classified by type and strength of storm. Major U.S. catastrophes, future and unclassified.

Elsie
and Henry

Elsie A. Prisk looks slowly down at her foot pressing hard on the brake pedal as her 1980 Ford Fairmont station wagon slides diagonally through a stop sign, burying a portion of its front end in the opposing snowbank. She is on her way to the Cane Funeral Home in Baraga and will now be late to the funeral service of her friend, Nina. Elsie had seen the obituary in the paper, and she was struck absolutely still by the fact that she did not know until it was in print. There was a terrible way in which the words *Nina Poirier* did not resemble the woman she knew, only ten years her elder, who died at seventy-one in the hospital. Elsie's mother said—a year before she herself died—that as you age, you get used to this constant sense of loss, the growing tally, but Elsie never has. Whether due to natural cause, accident, or murder, she thinks it doesn't get easier, especially on the young or involving them (so many recently it seems: her Liz, never far from her mind, especially in the winter; that other girl brutal in the paper). The obituary did not give the specific reason for her death, though Elsie went through it four times. She wondered whether the casket would be open.

She looks at the snow covering the corner of her windshield and blinks. She tries an arm to see if it will move. It does, and by repeating this same process on other parts of her body, she understands that her body is still intact and functional—a whole and useful thing. She counts the movements of her pulse against the second hand on her watch, even though she feels fine, lucid even, ten years younger. Elsie is—or used to be—a medical technician at Marquette Memorial Hospital and understands the quiet signals the body gives off, proof of its continued importance. Her pulse is fast, over a hundred beats a minute, but everything seems to be in order. She looks at her hatbox, gray and empty on the floor, and hopes that it is not damaged.

Elsie hears a knock on the rear window and turns her body with her head, so that she sees a man's breath coming in visible puffs against the glass, fogging it up. She waits for his announced intention. He seems concerned.

She reaches over to unlock the passenger-side front door, and the man (he's quite ugly!) asks if she is all right. She says she thinks she is.

"Do you want me to call the police?" he wants to know.

"No, that won't be necessary." Elsie is about to climb over to the door, but he stops her, says hold on, that she's in there good, and that he'll dig her out.

So it is all right. Elsie watches as he retreats out of her vision, and she watches the space he left behind for a moment, hoping he will return. In a minute, he does return, and with a rusted metal shovel in his right hand. She watches as he approaches.

"Try to turn on the car. I'll get rid of some of this snow."

"All right." Elsie knows that her words are clearer than her mind right now, and wonders if she might be in shock. She turns the key in the ignition, but at first it won't turn over. She waits a minute, careful not to flood the engine, and tries again. This time it comes to life, sputtering at first in the snowy cold covering the hood of her car, then she revs the engine, roaring loudly, surprising her so much she takes her foot off the gas. The sound quiets, and she can hear the shovel making contact with the metal on the side of her car.

He comes to the door, "Sorry about that. I don't think I scratched you up any."

She watches the sweat curl in rivulets down his neck. "It's okay."

He disappears again into her windshield, and there is a shovel motion, pulling heaps of white onto the road beside the car. After several long blank minutes inside, where it is so warm she could sleep (but she knows better—this could be it, her clock's last tick, she knows; she has to keep awake to see what happens), he reappears and says, "Okay, you should be good to go."

Elsie feels a sense of slow gratitude, but before she can say anything, he is gone, and soon a car door slams. She looks at the hand-print he left on the icy window, already beginning to fill in with frost. Her breath catches and returns.

She looks down at her hands in surprise, and wonders how much time has passed. She checks her pocketwatch, which is gold-inlaid ivory, now illegal to import, a friend had told her. It reads quarter of four. She looks up to the sun as it begins its descent into the evergreen-framed horizon—it goes down so early this far North and this deep in the year. She is already late; she checks her hatbox once again and backs her car out onto the street, feeling good again, alive and heedless of what might be approaching from behind.

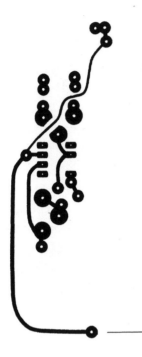

Dear, distance is a hush, a shush
a glass of milk
delivered through the ether
like a dose ——————

Commercial Systems

C risco, the snow is there for you to move through to get to church or wherever else you're meant to be: the mall, downtown at Commercial Systems where your sister's waiting for you to choose a Christmas present for your stepdad whom neither of you live with and who is obsessed with office supplies. Which explains the interest in Commercial Systems which is the only purveyor of quality papers and stationery in town, not to mention their vast sticker collection—scratch and sniffs being your favorite with their creepy chemistry when you were younger. Your sister, Carrie, is waiting in the snow—maybe admiring its patterns as it turns around her on the sidewalk in front of the store like a carousel or like some mathematical form—getting colder and colder, her cheeks taking on red like a ship takes on water as it lists in the canal. There are so many capsized hulls at the bottom of Portage Lake and the canal that cuts the Keweenaw Peninsula off from the rest of Upper Michigan. Many ships have gone down in winter storms or summertime in the body of water that is Lake Superior. Why do we say *body of water*, you wonder, as your sister gets colder and colder and might decide to go in without you, and you're still not moving; it's only a mile walk across the bridge to the other side of the canal to meet her in the city that is a twin of the one you're in but further south. But you're strangely fixed in place in your driveway watching similar snow patterns to what your sister is seeing. The weather is a system of surprise. The weather is a ghost of a body that used to be there. The weather is shreds of fact assembled into precipitation. The weather is retribution for what you've done wrong.

Carrie will go into the store though she knows you hate it when she does that, because then you get nervous and sometimes won't even go in, but you know how she is and she won't wait—freezing—outside for long. You had better go. You had better or she'll be angry and maybe your stepdad won't get a present and he'll be angry, too.

But you can see the canal from here, the canal that holds the bodies of snowmobilers and the men who manned the *Ranger I* and *Ranger II*, the cruise ships that tote campers out to Isle Royale, the eye in the wolf's head that is Superior. The cruise ships that sank, or so you've been told, before the construction of the current ship, the *Ranger III*. The canal holds the last thoughts of many grievers whose men have gone through the ice, or been lost in thunder. It holds the bodies of teenagers who jump off the lift bridge for kicks because what else is there to do for kicks. It holds the future, murdered girl and all. It holds your future anger and years of constant loss and need for revenge. It will hold the remains of the high school once it is condemned, once it is demolished and discarded bit by bit into the water. It holds nothing of the gorgeous symmetry that your sister always talks about. It holds a killer and a lover. It holds your future dreams of vandalism. It holds those who wouldn't go out to Misery Bay to deface the dredge with spray-paint cans that rattled like pneumonia in your lungs.

The Organization
and Formation of Blizzards
as Seen by Satellites: N–Z

N ever be too prepared. Never respond to frostbite by immersing the affected limb in hot water (use cold, then lukewarm). Never going outside is one method of dealing with the erratic weather. Never leave bread crumbs as a marker for your trail. Or, never tell your wife what you did when you were young. Or, further, never do what you tell your wife you'll never do. Or, perhaps, do and tell her everything, every last chore or minor injury. Path you left through the snow at her aunt's house after you shoveled through the night. Path of your departure from and return to your marriage. Path your son took after he killed that girl. Path of your son back from what is far beyond your worst nightmare, cliché as that may sound. Path which you must take to find a way to either forgiveness or forgetfulness brought on by drink or by submission to the weather. Paths of ETCs during June 1993 over the US. Paths of snowstorms tracking over the body of Upper Michigan. Paths of cars slid off the roads into the snowbank are easy to find for the first hour of the storm. Quiet, now, just listen to the coming down. Quietnesses alone or with your family are of different qualities. Quietly down the stairs during the night to finish off the tortellini in the fridge. Roof failure in the barn collapse during the big winter of 1979 coincided with your mother's death and left a mark. Roof failure is the worst betrayal of the safety pact that your building of the house against the storm outside secured. Schematic of one possible cause for wind shifts occurring ahead of temperature changes in cold frontal passages. Schematic diagram showing the manner through which heavy snowfall can be produced from low pressure systems tracking southeasterly along the coast. Schematic diagram illustrating the overall flow fields within and the organization of spring snowstorms in the lee of the Rocky Mountains. Schematic diagram illustrating the large-scale 100-50 kPa thickness patterns associated with snow/ice pellet storms as opposed to freezing rainstorms. The insurance industry. The insurance industry and its methods for combating fraud. The insurance premiums go up each year as you move closer to potential death. The life insurance that you doubled on yourself and on your wife a year ago weighs heavily on your mind. Underneath the policy you wonder what life insurance means in all its morbidity. Underneath the snow caking on the roof, it's warm inside thanks to fire and no lack of love in spite of all your marriage's faults and the fault lines that mark it from the inside. Underneath it all you both have your secrets and you keep them close to your hearts like children. Vulnerability, yours, to winter storms. Vulnerability to unexpected changes such as death, dismemberment, or crippling emotional failure. Vulnerability to sudden shifts in air pressure. Vulnerability, field assessments. Warnings of your vulnerability to all these things, and insurance against potential collapse. Warnings of winter storms. Warnings of extension of the season. Warning against eating the rest of the tortellini in the fridge during the night, expressed in verse on note attached to the Tupperware. Warnings, generally ignored. Warnings, ignored, resulting in loss of fingertips due to accidents or exposure to fire or cold. Warnings, broadcast, emergency tones. Warnings, social aspects. Your fault, your family. Your son. Your lack of forethought. Your end and emptiness. Your cold and brittle fingers. Your trees outside—the ones you planted—stiff with sheaths of ice and soon to break. Zero, time to blizzard and other forms of necessary impact.

Forecast

I is not about the leather jackets or the letter jackets or the sun that gleams off the hood of his Trans Am as it arrives in a cloud of dust like the beginnings of a blizzard. It's not about the shoplifted jewelry or the supply of illicit alcohol—although all of these are factors, like wind plus precipitation plus humidity plus pressure equals weather. It is the private tenderness that makes Bone irresistible, a force of season, like something that must be dealt with, relished, and melted off afterward, if you're so lucky to hold out until spring. It is the spray-painted slogans on the overpasses—not just the message but the branding and the fact of them. All this is why Carrie ends up reclined in the passenger side of the high school burnout dropout counselor's-nightmare's car, which is not a Trans Am like she says, but a Camaro (she watches but sometimes doesn't see it all), good as that or nearly as good.

All of this takes place in the weeks before the event, the watershed that divides, that splits, that cleaves the community in half for three years until the act is over and forgotten, buried in the ground like copper and in the papers for future crime historians.

Her friends, her teachers wonder: 760 verbal, 720 math, 34 composite ACT, AP English: 5, AP Physics B: 5. What in creation in all of God's green and terrified earth is Carrie doing with him? He's like a black hole for learning. Nothing comes back out, not light, not heat, not weight, not force, not moans, not words. Everything goes in and smolders there.

Maybe that is not the right metaphor, they concede—more like the cracked concrete of a wall gone through years of winter, taking nothing in, letting nothing out. Just showing the slim beginnings of a crack.

Is it that hard to understand attraction? Those who speak out against Bone, last name Lumberg, true first name: Kelvin, not remembered except on typed forms (school, tax, MIP, emancipation of a minor) and filed in the records room that used to be a janitorial closet on the bottom floor, with the ancient groaning boiler—do the teachers, the concerned members of the community remember the rush of days when they were seventeen? How everything was filled with light or darkness or what's in-between, what blurs? How could this boy—this man, let's face it, at least legally—be attractive to a girl like Carrie whom they call girl, young woman at most, always innocence, never woman, never lady. He is a symbol of all the wrong turns, wrong things. He is undesirable like bleach on jeans, like dust, like muck and motor oil staining the collars of your shirts, on clean white countertops just installed by Sears.

In spite of (or because of) her love of numbers and the patterns they suggest, Carrie is slowly becoming a statistic. On top of all the other numbers (height, weight, bust, waist, hips) she will before long be a victim, partially by choice, it would appear. We will refer to her and those like her in Sociology and Civics classes for years thereafter. A number of words in the paper, on the evening news. Look at her move through the halls out into the world on open lunch—she's more than half number already, but lovely, like ice cream on metal, bird in air.

Does she know that she's becoming story, warning beacon?

o

Bone takes her out to the breakers where Lake Superior funnels down into the body of the Portage Canal that divides the Keweenaw Peninsula—home to all the dead mines this far North like hollow roots into the earth—from the rest of Michigan, from the rest of the world.

Bone takes her to the abandoned mine shafts that he has uncovered, torn back the doors, hacked out the locks, opened up the yawn within. This yawn means silence, isolation, means veins of ore. It once meant profit, immigration. Now that's something she won't see elsewhere unless she takes one of the mine tours down inside. The tours for tourists—the dilution of the mine experience (the twelve-hour days of total sound and char, dark air and root and blackness) into an hour-long trip down a passageway that has been determined to be structurally safe. This is something new—a real danger—that she is privy to alone. He shows her his father's gun, his off-brand cigarettes bought from the Reservation down in Baraga for cheap. Even the gasoline he nozzles into the car can combust. She is seeing something lonely, naked, without packaging.

The teachers keep their windows open as long as they can into the winter to listen for the screams—*Just in case* they tell themselves, they tell themselves *We are vigilant,* they tell themselves *There is something we can do.* They keep canaries in small cages by the windows to scout for gas. They tune in the television to reruns of *Red Dawn* where the Commies invade and the kids are all that's left to save the country, where the kids take to the hills, and arm themselves. Even the Vice Principal is on alert—he knows Carrie's name (and numbers), and is terrified to see her go. He calls her parents, but gets politeness, thanks for calling, brushoff.

Even the weather speaks—thunderstorms come up from nowhere. Hail. Lightning. Tornado weather if this was tornado country, if the landscape would permit it.

The buildings move very slightly in the wind.

The concrete contracts as the temperature drops.

Miniskirts can still be worn, but with risk.

o

Bone takes her to the balcony in the movie theater, sneaks them past the velvet rope that says "Closed" and "Danger, Off Limits." Bone takes her to the movies. Bone is alone with her again in the dark on the balcony that's been declared structurally unsound doing who knows what. They are unsupervised, unchaperoned, alone. Hear their moaning.

What does Carrie have to say about this? She's stopped speaking entirely except to him. Her parents disapprove—but do they know where she's been taken by this man this big boy this set of arms and engine, this criminal in the making? What can they do but ground her, make sure she goes to class, lecture her, write a hundred times *I Will Not Sneak Out Again* in that neat handwriting of hers (one of many things left behind— lined paper evidence of this), slide pamphlets under her door with graphic photographs of venereal diseases and pregnancy statistics.

Tell her, you, about those who are bound for murder: Women, women alone in cars, women alone with men, women who are so caught up by men, sometimes the men themselves, women aged sixteen to thirty-six, and even older women. Measured numbered estimated women. Women who leave their homes. Women who leave their homes in the night. Women who date men who drive Trans Ams or cars they think are Trans Ams. Women who date men with guns. Women who care, women who crave. Women who are in the way of becoming part of something dangerous.

There are ways of reducing your murderability index. Spend more time with friends, girlfriends especially, cut yourself off from that awful boy. Ice-cream floats and matinees. The Sunday Church dance and meal thereafter.

Tell her all of this. That will make a difference.

It's the white desire—the thing that makes the Finns run from the saunas and jump into the snowbank. It's the need for something different— speed, the lack of seatbelts, the alcoholic killing of the liver, the killing of the lakes with cancer runoff from the processed ore, the impossibility and invincibility of the body held up against the rushing air. It's the jumping from the cliffs surrounding the waterfall into the pool below. It's the slow removal of clothes and the nakedness below, the body's warm steam into the air that says winter's coming.

All this will end so badly. In retrospect the police should have been called, forced to arrest Bone, arrest Carrie, put them in separate cells, keep them apart with bars and space and institutional food and all of the community's thoughts and cards and care.

All this will end in ink on newsprint, ink that bleeds off onto the hands under too much use. All this will end in ink in accidental overprinting on the press—the superimposition of the crime on the weather forecast page.

What to do. It's because of the boredom, the burden of the future that is approaching regardless of what you do. The future approaching like a man on skis with a rifle on his back. The future approaching like a father with a belt. The future approaching like the secrets of disease passed down through generations. The future approaching like the threat of bars on Saturday then church on Sunday—all that obliteration then damnation/salvation is a life but it is not a good one.

What nobody knows: Bone listens to everything. He is all ear, pure receptor. He takes it in, all the book-length information. All the warnings, admonitions, predictions, daily forecasts in the barbershop, in the paper. He accumulates like snow. He just doesn't give it back. He won't test well. He won't test at all. He refuses. This frustration, this refuse, this refusal is a danger to the world and its infrastructure (a word he knows though doesn't use). He is all reluctance, quiet, Hydrogen, pre-fission.

The textbooks say it, too—potential energy, kinetic energy, how one becomes the other. All those pages open on the desks during a high-school fire drill.

What nobody knows, take two: Carrie knows exactly what she's doing, in a way. This is more a choice than anyone can guess. Awful, yes. But still she can at least scent the future coming toward her like the point of a knife, like a rape scene in a movie, like the denouement of a story, like the last black act of a tragedy on stage. How much does she know and when does she know it is the question, is the operation.

Bone takes her to the stampsand plains, the gritty black leftovers from processed ore bordering the lake, does figure-eights with his car for her, burns some gas for her, says his own kind of prayer for her. Bone takes her to the body shop where he works some afternoons (Bone? Working?) and True Value hardware so she can see all the tools and what they can do besides cut and grind. Bone takes her to the liquor store with his fake ID to buy some beer, to buy some chew, some cigarettes, some candy cigarettes, too, for irony, some ammunition, some rubbers, and some gum. Bone takes her everywhere she has not yet been allowed to go. And isn't this good enough for her, for both of them?

Oh, Jesus, Orpheus, can't anything be done?

The winter moves toward them like a cloud. Like exhaust. Like story problem Train A leaves X.

If the town is a body is it moving.

If the two of them are energy are they still potential.

If the town is a cancer caused by the residue from the rocks in the lake is it expanding.

Everything is good and ends badly.

The radio plays Sabbath. Somebody at the Christian station has convinced the DJ that Black Sabbath is a holy band and no one has informed him of the joke. A boon for Bone and guys who drive Camaros or Trans Ams, who drive seatbeltless well above the posted speed limits, who like the edge of Sabbath, the minds and bodies of the former honor students, the attention of the flashbulb burst, the awful fascination of the town.

The bodies of the teachers are upright in their chairs—stiff like rabbits or rigor mortis. The television's on but isn't playing anything worth noting. Some channels are only showing snow meaning static hush not precipitation. The voyeurs are looking in the windows at the teachers, watching what they're watching (which is nearly nothing, now twice removed). The windows of the cars are fogged.

Do we all desire her, yes we do. She will be our sex, our salvation.
    Do we all desire him too?

The barometer drops on Bone and Carrie as they make out furiously in the Camaro parked down at the breakers again where there are no lights, where there are no lights for miles, where all there is are miles. Still it is as if we can all see, at least in retrospect—the scene soon to be well-flashbulb-lit and pored over in countless AP news releases. We will have our tiny glory—the sickness and the pleasure of reflection, of post-traumatic prediction. It is time for the murder, then the winter after.

———— *Dear, this distance is a balding scalp, a bridge, a dead end, deadened nerve, long-distance dedication, a sort of stroke and reassurance*

Bowling Balls Sent Down Through Windows From Overpasses That Stretch Like Spiderwebs Above

It's the natural thought: You, Bone, you brute, stand on the overpass, looking through the metal grid that sections off the world below—and ask yourself what sort of shears or metal cutters, or clippers could be bought or stolen from buses, would be required to reveal a patch through which a large and swirled object—a Galaxie 500-polished bowling ball, owned by *Lannie,* seeing that his name is engraved in the lacquer, bought from a garage sale for eighty cents, and hauled twenty-six blocks in a cherry red Radio Flyer wagon here from downtown; the ball itself fourteen pounds, and looking like swirled cream caught in a stop-time glaze. And you hold the ball in your hands which are not dark white though maybe exhibiting a casual tan; you grip it like you think a bowler might, with the one-two-three-slide coming up; with the Brooklyn-side strike coming up, with the 7-10 split conversion coming up, with the hook that pulls the ball from the gutter back to the pocket and spins the pins to the waxed floor coming up, the high five coming up and arm pump coming up, your feeling of worth coming up, you put the carrying case down with your other hand, and you time the cars as they pass by underneath. Some might suggest timing kills

113

the sport; that one might just let go without anger. But there is no anger here; no disappointment at the job you just lost, or the fight at school you have just run from, the bruises that mark your spine all the way down to your ass like a map, your woman who waits in the Camaro, the kid who has your name and the way you move but doesn't know you, whom you watch only from afar; you are not in distress and, no, your upbringing is not responsible, and no, the weather is not responsible, and no, your father and his anger, your mother and her leaving (however unintentional)—they are not responsible either, and no, even you're not responsible. There is, however, a certain calculation, a feeling of order that keeps cars speeding along the highway that borders the lake at eighty miles an hour no more than forty feet from each other, the rage that can build when you're in that car and some kid is skipping stones across the interstate like it was a slate gray lake, and one clicks across your windshield, spiderwebbing it because your car is so old it doesn't have auto glass, as you soon find out, though you didn't know there was such a thing as auto glass, auto glass that has a rubber coating so it breaks into squares and does not shatter, even under repeated blows from a hammer, you and Bernard and his brother demonstrating this in a field, creating arcs in the air with the sledgehammer you took from your father's toolshed and will not return. There is the force that holds the tire to the pavement, the body in the seat, the machines grinding in lines, the gears turning in a not unsurprising fashion, the viewer's limbs to the armrests and to the floors, the gauze to the blood to the body, the pin in the skin, the face to the pavement, the boot to the small of the back, the breath to the face, the heart to the fist, the lip to the lip, the light continually coming down like hot and awful rain upon the dirty hands of the earth; and how easily it can all be busted up like a crowd or a drunk, or cut apart like an artery, a vessel; it's like skin or a thin meniscus, the concave or convex fluid curve to the lip of the cup, how a tiny penny can cut it, and spill; and then your breath is half out like you were firing a .22 in Boy Scout Camp, at targets or ducks, or after school at squirrels, or at the storm windows in old Mrs. Ligon's house down the block, and how it is that you can cause an animal to cease its jitter and dance, and so you let go, and you watch, and the ball falls—like New Year's Eve—in slow motion in stop time like in water, or descending in vegetable oil, or into the slow water at the base of the Mariana Trench, and it hits or it doesn't, you become a headline or you don't, your father hit you or not, and this ends, or begins, and either way you should know we love you regardless of how things turn out.

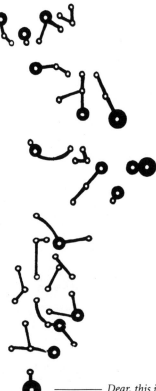

—————— *Dear, this is a mouth, a month, a moth*
emerging from, a cloth across the brow,
a going-North

Piñata

He had a piñata at his seventh-birthday party, Jelly remembers, sitting on the pot in the plane bathroom, which is not like his grandmother's pot at home with the padded seat that makes a whooshing air-release sound when you sit on it, which is to say it is not in any way comfortable. He would cry if he wasn't the one who finally smashed it open and let its candied guts rain down on the plastic tarp covering the living room carpet, so his parents eventually stopped letting others have their turns with the baseball bat. He remembers the exact feeling he had when swinging the bat the final time, his muscles having some prescient notion that this was it, the one to crack the donkey-shaped shell in half, and though he was blindfolded, he could still see out through the red handkerchief which hadn't been folded over enough times, and he watched the bat connect and the animal's back-half cave in. There were cheers as everybody scrambled for candy and moans of disappointment as Jelly covered it all with his body until everyone gave up and went home, mad, mad, mad.

The reason he's thinking of piñatas now is unclear. Thousands of feet above the weather that haunts the ground, he can feel the seat underneath him vibrating with every dip of the plane—and there are many dips of the plane since this is propeller, not a jet, and they're flying through and over a lot of excited air. There's a knock on the door. "Occupied!" he says, half-loud, but he isn't sure the person heard him, so he says it again, louder. He's trying as hard as he can to make it quick, but it's hard when you're rushing through the air above your home, arriving just in time for the funeral of your friend Carrie, whom you haven't spoken to in years, but when you heard the news, you knew you'd have to come.

He gets done, pretends to wash his hands for show—runs the water a bit just in case someone's listening—and feels the cool zip of air as the toilet flushes in its weird, vacuumy way. Getting out, there is a line outside which wasn't there before.

Someone else is sitting in his seat—which he'd fought so hard for before, to sit next to the pretty girl and not the sincerely obese couple on the other side.

With an "Um, excuse me!" he makes his point clear, but the man sitting there just ignores him and continues his attempt to pick up the girl sitting in the seat beside.

"Hello? This is my seat."

The man seems annoyed, and gets up, as the girl is now ignoring him and trying to read an issue of *Condé Nast* that another traveler must have left behind. Jelly sits back down, says, "Wow, that guy was cheesy."

"Tell me about it," she spits back, putting down the magazine. She starts saying how she likes flirting with guys but not with old thirty-plus men with greasy hair and cowlicks, and how she's got three boyfriends at home whom she sees alternately, and who are not aware of the others' existence.

He says his name's Jelly, and hers is . . . ? "Sandy. Sandy. I'm glad you came back because that gross old guy reminded me of my father who used to beat me."

Jelly is slowly figuring things out, realizing that she's lying, maybe has been all along, lying to that strange man and everyone else in the airport and airplane. So he lies, too, tells her about his crazed abusive stepfather who used to keep him and his two nonexistent brothers' heads in the toilet if they came home late or with the wrong amount of change, and they get in this long conversation about abusive relationships, without either one of them really revealing anything true. They talk for the rest of the flight in energetic, high-pitched tones, each one feeling a little like trying to break their conversation down and say one true thing, letting it fall down to a real level, where things matter, but not really getting how to get over the blindfolds they're both wearing, how to see through their red fabric, how to swing the bat in the right direction, at the right angle into the air to hit and pop it open, and watch everything sweet and wrapped inside fall out all over their carpets or protective, translucent plastic tarps.

Dream Obits
for My Mother

Who my X my other.

Who my gone-again my postcards from another country.

Who my most.

Whose mint is planted in the front yard.

Whose mint we pick and roll between our fingers.

Whose scent is here familiar like a song on the radio.

Who can be used for tea.

Whose name is writ in bags below the shed.

Who married an engineer.

Whose notes I keep finding in books with flowers in Contact paper.

Whose items have all been auctioned off or disposed of by now.

Whose caricature is etched in glass in the living room.

Who expired on the green-striped couch.

Who would never say it like that.

Who is both answer and question, hole and whole, till and until.

Who is in another country where they search you at the border.

Who told the story about going across to Canada on the International Bridge and being stopped by Customs.

Who wondered if there even is a Canada.

Who wondered what Boxing Day was.

Who changed all of her currency into Canadian.

Who an anagram for how.

Who liked short hair and English.

Who can only be discovered after death like the best secret.

Who kept recipes.

Who kept my father straight and here.

Who writes periodically, I know.

Whose letters are no longer carried by the post.

Who can be described in air as both mother and wife, confidant.

Who could get a long-distance dedication.

Who was worth and worthy.

Who is overture. Who is over.

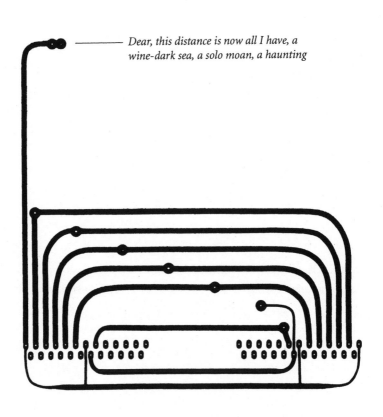

*Dear, this distance is now all I have, a
wine-dark sea, a solo moan, a haunting*

Teeth

Timothy's teeth felt like they were shattering again. He was washing his hands, running them under the warm water, letting the pink soap rinse away. With his hands now totally immersed in the liquid, he could picture his head crashing against the sink and his teeth smashing like glass, spreading into splinters and careening into the sides of his fleshy mouth. He watched his toothshards flying in slow motion, wheeling and turning like strange compasses, a sharp, expanding cloud of enamel and glass.

The splashing sound of water on the bathroom's linoleum floor and the run of water down his leg kicked Timothy back into reality, and he quickly turned off the two calcium-spotted chrome handles. The entire sink was filled with soapy water, not sudsy or foamy now but just translucent and runny. His hands were dripping water on his jeans, and he lowered himself to the exact level of the water. It came just above the lip of the sink, threatening to spill if jiggled, but for now, the surface tension was enough to keep it in place.

Timothy, however, couldn't just leave a sink full of water in a public restroom. His sister would be angry. She hated wasting water. He couldn't keep the door locked forever; people would want to come in sooner or later. He had to get the water level in the sink lowered, and the only way to do it was to pull out the bright green stopper in the bottom of the sink, which would involve having to plunge his skinny hand into the water and spilling more on the floor. He felt his insides turn ninety degrees at the thought; the sound of the splashing water, the feel of the liquid running down the sides, spreading into a pool at the base of the sink.

He knelt and considered the underside of the sink briefly, following the two copper pipes running down the base of the sink into the rectangular holes in the floor like hammered snakes. He put his hand on the left pipe, taking its temperature. It was chilly and he could feel the condensation between his fingertips when he drew them back. He lay down in the cool puddle on the striped linoleum and looked at the two thin white pipes running along the ceiling. They were smooth and round, labeled *Domestic water in, Domestic water out,* like arteries carrying dark blood to some churning white muscle. The artificial lighting did not speak to his heart.

He had a tooth pulled two weeks ago, tugged out by some dentist's tool, given to him in a pink envelope. It wasn't uniform and perfect white like he had pictured it, smooth and rounded. It was yellowish brown and more like a lump of soft luminescent coal, bumpy and amorphous. It seemed so foreign to him, like it didn't come from his mouth at all, but from someone else's. He reached into his pocket and pulled out a handful of old laundry detergent. It reminded him of the beach, how even the earth itself was not solid, how his feet could be held up by tiny grains of sand. He thought of sitting on the beach, on the edge of the water, where the sand was wet and cold. The water would wash up over his knees, and if he sat there long enough, it would soon wash up to his neck, so only his head was above water, and his eyes would follow the lapping waves. He brought his hand up to eye level, and let the speckled powder spill over the sides and onto the floor like water over dikes.

His parents—when they were together—used to own a collection of tourist books, a comprehensive guide to Europe and the Middle East. He was too young to understand any of the English words or commonplace phrases in French or German, but he would stare at the covers splashed across with colorful flags of countries. When he was nine and could understand some of the text, he read that, at any given time, half of the Netherlands was below sea level.

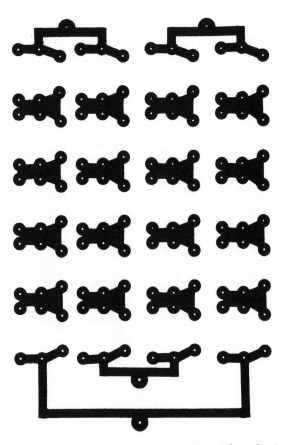

—————— Dear, I hope that is enough

Consideration
of the Force Required
to Break an Arm

Crisco, consider this: dropping a full can of soda from the top of a three-story stairwell into a trash basket on the bottom. Assume the can is full and still closed. Assume you bought it and meant to buy diet cause you're trying to cut down on your sugar intake since you read about the problems that it can cause somewhere, but that the machine—damn! damn!—gave you Coke instead. Assume that the most significant relationship in your life up until now just ended and you're feeling bitter and somehow callous. Assume you have no real scruples about dropping the can to the trash basket three stories below as a sort of game—can you make it the bin, or can't you? Will the can explode once it hits? Assume that the trash is empty (doesn't it look like a toothless mouth?) and will make a hugely hungry boom of a sound when and if the can makes it in. Assume that there is no wind resistance because you're inside. Assume that there will be no foreign objects in the way of your shot. Forces to consider include: gravity (a = 9.8 m/sec² on earth; atmospheric pressure = 14.8 foot-pounds/inch at sea level), and the force with which you chuck the can. Assuming you let go without exerting additional force to accelerate the can on the way down, and assuming you've calculated the angle correctly, and assuming a story is equal to about fifteen feet in this building (assume this building is built with six-foot-tall people in mind with an appropriate amount of space above for light fixtures, sound insulation, piping that runs between the floors and carries the hot and cold water in and out of each bathroom—men's and women's, though it's hard to tell which is which, and sometimes you've confused the two, much to your embarrassment) how long will it take for the can to enter the empty trash below? Assuming you drop the can without exerting additional force on it, how fast will it be moving when it enters the trash? Assume that you don't mean to do anyone any harm, and that this is the province of math, the hypothetics and mechanics of motion, force, and impact. Assume that this takes place in a vacuum though of course nothing ever really does, does it? Assume that you came from a stable family that didn't split up when your sister was—again this is so awful—raped and killed. Assume that the shock and grief of her departure didn't rip your *mather* and *fother* apart, even so much so that they changed their titles with regard to the family, not being mother and father but *mather* and *fother*. Assume they could get past whatever personal differences they had with respect to grief, and with respect to coping with grief, not with getting over it exactly because you can never really get over it (and what is it? a fucking hill?), but they managed Kubler-Ross's stages of grief. Assume that two rational people could handle what this is: a sort of tragedy, senseless, another good girl lost, et cetera. Assume that relationships are built to last. Assume that the poisoning of the water in a marriage only affected the *mather* and *fother*'s relationship with each other, and assume the remaining kid was part of a different system entirely unaffected, unredirected by this. Assume that your girlfriend hadn't redelivered your belongings through registered mail with return-receipt which required you to fucking sign for them so she would get the confirmation back. Assume you were not to blame for this split. Assume that your parents' busted marriage had nothing to do with forecasting your lack of luck with women. Assume that your brother's death has nothing to do with your dislike of ice and winter sports. Assume that men and women are meant to be together. Assume that men and men, women and women, are meant to be together. Assume you (or anyone else in your position) might love again. Assume that actions, again, do not take place in a vacuum but assuming otherwise makes problems much easier to graph and solve. Assume there is only one variable at any given time that can be solved for and understood. Assume that—really!—it is not in your head to break the arm of a girl you do not know. Assume that you can cease to think, that the brain can stop its petty operation. Assume you can relearn to mull. Will the force and accumulated velocity of the can upon reaching the interjected arm of a passing girl who you do not yet know and could never (you believe) come to love you after this incident, could never understand the complicated motivation and sequence of events that led to this event (though keep in mind the margin of error), could never visualize the series of compulsions and activations that are you think like tiny boats, each laden with candles, set down all the way across the water in a line, on a canal, at dusk, and viewed from a couple hundred feet away, or up above from the bridge—could never visualize the insane and completely untouchable beauty of this line in this moment (which will soon be completely bungled by a million variables all buzzing and kicking and doing whatever they do when you're not looking), and, more importantly, could never learn to see the way you do, because everybody's blind and tied up, and sunk to the bottom as if wrapped in piñatas that never found the party at which their presence was expected, and were subsequently dropped off in the lake. How much force can that can exert upon a white and uncorroded arm?

Stop
Your Crying

Come on. Leave this place. Buck and buckle up. Make your way North through the border to Thunder Bay. Find a name your name your mother's name your family name on the list of radio epitaphs in the books or on the Internet. Listen in on this conversation. Clip your handset to the junction box and become part of a family. Eavesdropping always works like this, to make you part of something. Listen to how they talk—the fact that they talk in English or in French, your heart's language. Listen to any mention of anyone named Crisco or Liz, any mention of armlessness or loss. Anything relating to glossy magazine photos or pictures in the paper. Any words between lovers or trace of God in the telephone line. Listen to the hush when the words are done. After the hang-up, the dropping of the carrier, the trunk is yours to use, to coast through to Florida in the wire where there is sun and everything is life-size and stuffed like an animal or an envelope. Take on everything you hear. Just don't speak or they'll know you're there. Let the tone guide you down the rabbit hole et cetera. Let the pitch and squeal of faxes and modems connecting inform your grief. The wire connects you to Florida, your extended family, and anyone in Canada.

You can dial up dead Liz or Crisco's murdered sister Carrie. You can dial your armless brother's arms. You can touch-tone your way back to fire. You can fool the fools at Michigan Bell and tunnel out. You can encode your name in silence and rings of wire. Enter your name with the touch-tone keys and see who that gets you. Dial 313 which means lower Michigan or 906 which is your code or 616 which gets you by the east edge of Lake Michigan. The dial is lit like a fire like a hearth above a fire covered with candles and maybe some Christmas shit. The fire is hot and sparks come out through the fire screen though they're not supposed to. The newspaper used to start the fire is black and bits float in the air: *ings* and halves of words, the conjugations and vowels. If you breathe you might get the burned ends of language in your lungs or in your heart or in the billion capillaries, the cords that tie the spine to the thigh, to the cochlea where you keep your balance, the mechanics of the middle ear, the throat so sore, the singing sinus, or one of the other important cavities of the body.

Constellations

1 / Orion: What do you do with the things you don't understand?

Timothy looked over his shoulder and wiped his nose with his fist, maybe. Memory was not completely reassuring. His eyes swiped from side to side, waiting for the gray cat with the white star pattern to appear. The way it moved, materialized, from out of the dark, he wasn't sure it actually existed, but it always snuck up on him anyway. It would appear from behind the collapsed barn and stutter-step toward the round tire with the lint nest. It slept there sometimes, and sometimes slept somewhere else. He didn't know where exactly, but he supposed that it lived in a bed of dark ferns which lacerated its body with continuous nighttime motion.

He listened for the reports of fireworks from the sky up above. He counted each one as it was fired toward the stars, and mentally checked it off as it exploded, probably throwing whirling fingers of light downward to earth. He never watched them, because he was afraid of their fiery tails. So, technically, he was never absolutely sure they went off. But that was irrelevant. His mind whirred and shifted, then ground to an asthmatic halt. His father was at home, fingering an empty inhaler, maybe wondering where he was, maybe not. For the last two weeks, Timothy had come out here any night he could and sat in the bus, with his pellet gun squeezed between his thighs or resting on the seat beside him, waiting for the cat.

Sometimes he would look up at the sky, thinking about astronomy and gas giants, and sometimes he would prop up empty paint cans on the rotted fence, and sometimes he would shoot them. When he shot them, they would totter and rim, then fall slowly to the ground. His mind was a camera with cheap, slow film.

He didn't always shoot the cans, though. He enjoyed watching the twilight absorb these sentinels, disbelieving their existence past the limits of his sight. When he returned, he was always surprised to find them still balancing on the fence, where he left them. Then he would probably shoot them, if he felt like it. If he shot them, he would find more to set up before going home.

Some nights, he would gaze at the sky and make up his own constellations. Constellations, he thought, were made up by someone originally, just pulled together out of essentially nothing. If you looked at the diagrams of constellations in old fat books and thin, bleachy magazines, it was clear that they did not make much intrinsic sense. People at some point had just projected their own images onto the stars. The pictures pushed onto stars were sharp and alien, and didn't smell natural to Timothy at all. He thought that maybe it was comforting to look at the dark wideaway blackness and see something familiar: patterns of stars; so he made his own. *Asshole*, he called one. This was a somewhat-perfect ring of stars in the middle of a wide open space, and the first thing that came to mind was exactly that. Another one was *Angelfish*, because it resembled one to him, and *Black Wrench*, because this one was not really a constellation, but an absence of stars that looked like a wrench, more or less. "More or less," he said sometimes, which didn't make any real sense, but that's what his dad said, "I'll be home at eight, more or less." "Oh, you'll be fine—more or less." "Quit your crying—you're a fucking man, more or less." To Timothy, more or less often meant just less.

The clearing in which the bus rested resembled an island. Timothy imagined the aerial view. From this perspective, the forest-sea would cut away into an oblong, elliptical, maybe even egglike clearing. The grass was short and white in the summer, when it grew, as if affected by chemicals. It resembled an angel's razor-stubble; certainly not his dad's, dark and cutting on his skin. This white color made the contrast between the darkness of the foliage, the whiteness of the short grass, and the yellow-beige of the bus all the more distinct and resonant. It seemed to Timothy that, through the sun's constant pressure on the layers of yellow paint, the bus seemed to be assimilating quickly toward the bleached color of the grass. He would sit on this bus sometimes during hard nights, and that's where he sat now.

He felt his butt beginning to solidify and cramp. He moved, and it hurt. It felt like he was paralyzed, stuck to the hard, textured plastic, the kind they always have on buses. Green and useless, avocado and spit. He didn't move and instead cut holes in the back of the bus seats as he had other nights, holes in the shapes of stars and crescent moons and what he imagined comets to look like. Timothy had never seen a comet, but he was familiar with the popular conception of them, the pictures he saw in *Time*. He pulled out his knife and flipped out the longer of the two blades, and sunk it into the pea-green-colored seat backing. He felt some resistance at first, and then it slipped in deeper with a tiny rush, and hit the metal frame with a light dry click. He carved the shape of a star into the seat back, and tried to pull the piece out. Because it wouldn't come at first, he moved his head closer, so that he could feel the chill of the plastic on his cheek, and used his teeth. Gritting together his molars, he pulled hard and back. At the moment it finally gave, he felt a sense of weightlessness, a momentary surge of adrenaline and recognition, then he hit the back of his head on the window.

Timothy always sat in the back of the bus for some reason, a vague sense of alienation maybe, remembering weeks spent on other buses on the way to school, watching his sister Harriet and her friend Liz, glossy, glowering, glancing at boys, sucking secretly on cigarettes. He really didn't know, or give much thought to it. The bus had been here for as long as he could remember. He was walking through the woods with his pellet gun, shooting at grouse and rabbits but not really hitting any, and he saw it in a clearing, surrounded by huge, water-filled tractor tires, where bugs lived on hot days. It was up on blocks in the front, and the back had a flat tire which hung limply around the hubcap, and oddly enough, one good tire on the back right. It was a *Bluebird*, with the huge mirror for the bus driver to see what was going on both on the road and inside the bus, and two convex mirrors sticking out on the sides to watch the road. Those were the first things he broke, and then most of the other windows, except the windshield and rear window. He found emergency flares in a metal compartment behind the driver's seat, and he set them off for no articulable reason, other than to watch them burn. Timothy originally thought they might explode, like sticks of dynamite, but they didn't—they just burned brightly for a while, then died. He was disappointed.

The bus was partly rusted on the outside, and in a few places, he could see the ground through the floor. Timothy avoided these spots because of the deck incident. His sister's friend, Jesse, had been pacing in circles on his wooden deck, and his foot came down on a rotted spot, a sinkhole in the wood, and instead of encountering the solid floor of the deck, it continued through, pulling his entire leg into a wooden netherworld. Timothy's memory rewound and freeze-framed on the image of Jesse's face just as groin hit wood—a look of profound disbelief and confusion, an empty milk-cup shattering quietly on linoleum. He felt let down even thinking about it. Sometimes, now, Timothy dreamed of rotting wood, balconies and floorboards, and would wake up with a splitting pain in his leg, which, though it went away with examination, never really left him. He felt dark all over and covered with a sticky, oppressive haze.

The bus rested next to a collapsed barn. Or, at any rate, he assumed it was a barn from looking through its moss-sticky treasures: old wheels and sheets of serrated metal, gears brown and paper-thin with rust, old chicken-wire and gray wooden hutches that creaked sometimes in the wind. There were plenty of objects, though, that he couldn't fit into place in his mind. He imagined some of them might have been dangerous in some way, but now they were all decayed or tarnished, rusted or destroyed, some bent and some flat-out broken. He enjoyed ordering and stacking the gears he found in piles. There were far too many gears. This was not easily explainable with his farmhouse hypothesis. He spread out the gears sometimes into the shapes of his made-up constellations, or just symmetrical patterns on the ground. He would press them into the dirt and then remove them, examining their imprints. He tried to think of the difference between the originals and the imprints, but nothing clicked. He looked at the empty spaces formed by the teeth of the gears, and then he contemplated the gears themselves, but couldn't reliably say what the difference was. It bothered him in some way, but he pushed it down and forgot.

He sat up and waited for the cat he had named *Orion*, waited for it to come so he could shoot it. When his breath began to freeze and the rear window of the bus became wet with moisture, he went home.

2 / Televisions in Jacuzzis: Somewhere along the line, the message gets lost.

Timothy dreamt alone in a bed as wide open as the dry, cracked skin of the plains. His fingers, in this dream, were whirling in patterns, over and over. They would close in on his face, then veer out and skip over the flat, cold mattress. They moved with a sense of self-will, tracing letters in English and Greek. He dreamed himself cutting bright green ribbons in a world made up of tiny tiles. The tiles were not noticeable—they seemed part of something bigger—unless he pushed his eye up close to them. Then they would become obvious, discrete. He tried to poke holes in the tiled surfaces with his whirling fingers. He slowly built himself into a small room and found there was a Jacuzzi there with a television blazing below the foaming, churning surface of the water. There were images on the television, but it was not distinguishable exactly what they were. A low moan of sound slowly emanated up from the bright set, but Timothy could not hear what it said. He had to interpolate from the hazy images he could see, turning them into the closest-fitting picture he had in his mind, pictures of bulldozers and frontloaders shoveling dirt into circles. The indistinguishable sound fit into this scheme as the consistent whine of their churning mechanical hearts. His father was in the corner now, finishing the wall with dark plaster and colored bricks.

3 / Maps and freckles: Can you show me the way home?

Timothy came back the next day with an old, red briefcase. He sat down quietly in the bus and pulled out a handful of maps. Some he had stolen from his dad's *National Geographic* collection—the only reason his dad subscribed to the magazine was for these maps. His dad had plastered and indexed over 100 maps on the walls, ceiling, and floor of their living room. He had fit them together in such a way that the maps formed an almost continuous representation of the world, except in the inverse. Walking in there felt like entering a self-contained universe, complete with its own inverse latitudes, longitudes, poles. It was an incredible thought that the world could be mapped, that there was no spot left on the planet that did not have its shape recorded on paper. It pushed Timothy a little left of himself to even think of the concept of mapping anything at all. How did experience become translated into these bright colors and borders, topographically defining a common existence? It hurt to think too much about the idea. When things hurt too much to think about, Timothy would pull a blue ballpoint pen out of his loose shorts and begin connecting the whorls on his fingers. His father would shift his lips and disapprove.

Timothy had stolen the maps from his father's collection, where he had doubles, and had brought them to the bus. He methodically licked the backs of each map and placed them, saliva-wet, on the walls of the bus, covering up the shattered windows. It took a good amount of spit, but they stayed, papier-mâchéd onto the inside of the bus. The maps were of New Zealand and ancient Mesopotamia, the Dead Sea and the Arctic Circle, the Pacific Northwest states and Hawaii. They formed a discontinuous representation of the world, but that was good enough for Timothy. He was fascinated with Yakutsk and Irkutsk, two divisions of land in Northeastern Asia where nothing seemed to be. He looked at his skin, so blank and white, hairless and unmapped. He wondered where his sister was. He fingered the chilly metal of the pellet gun on the seat next to him.

His eyes unfocused on the gun and Timothy just looked at its shape, sort of a black and brown crescent, tried to map it in his mind without focusing in on it, imagined it as a piece of land somewhere in the Black Hills of the Dakotas. Satellites had mapped it, certainly, but no one had ever really explored it, save the gawking, wheeling birds that skidded in the air currents over the slopes of its shiny black cliff faces and cold, rough brown hills.

His eyes focused again and he picked up the pistol and squinted in through the sight at each map, looking for population centers or mountain ranges. When he found one, he squeezed the trigger and popped a hole in the paper, letting in a tiny slanted pinprick of light. He shot holes in all of the maps and put the gun down, resting back and surveying the pattern that he had punctured in the topology. It was almost like stars in a way; he could form constellations from the holes. He traced the lines between points with his fingers and gingerly felt each hole, separately weighing each. What if, he thought, the holes were the stars, the defining points of the world, and everything in between was fiction?

Timothy remembered when he was eight and he had freckles. He had always had freckles, but that summer, they took on the appearance of something else. That was the summer they had left the glassless window that California was for him. His freckles had knotted themselves together in herds and congregations on his face. They were malignant, like clotting, swarming red blood cells on the surface of the skin. The doctor had said that it was not dangerous, but that Timothy's face needed to be kept clean and that he should stay out of the sun. He had to stay inside all summer, except during the twilight hours and the nights in which his father would sit up and point the constellations out to him. "See those three stars in a line? That's Orion, the archer. That's his belt."

The freckles had receded from a connected, communal mass to discrete, lonely spots, but not quite gone away. Some nights, Timothy would sit up, looking at his own face in the mirror, or a piece of broken glass, and would connect the dots with a felt-tip pen. He could imagine the wet sliver tongue of the pen, sliding across the pores on his face, connecting the freckles in the shapes of mountains, fish, and triggers. A trigger looked very much like a static, upside-down wave on his forehead. He fashioned a set of lips on his right cheek, all made of connected freckles. He drew shapes over and over, superimposing them on top of one another, until no single shape could be made out, but a conglomeration of black ink coated his face and made it heavy. The smell would finally overwhelm his nostrils and he would try to wash it out. He could get most of it, but it was still noticeable sometimes in the bright daylight, though his father never seemed to see it.

Now, Timothy looked outside through the hole in Papua New Guinea and saw Orion moving slowly up to the huge tire. If the tire was an angry, hungry mouth, the white teeth would slowly rise from the rubber gums, and the black lips would snap closed on the cat as it jittered its way up the tongue. He watched for a while as Orion circled jerkily around the tire. The cat was innocent, bright, unaware. Timothy slowly moved his finger up to the map of New Zealand and widened one of the holes to make room for the barrel of the gun. His eyelashes quivered softly, like lips, and he held his breath as his shaking fingers mapped the handle of the gun.

He remembered reading fragments of a story from a *National Geographic* about the mating habits of some aboriginal tribe in Australia. Most of the story had been lost, but he was able to pick up on the leftover bits: the blue paint they used to stripe their shins, the soft clucking sound the men made when approaching women, the spider-shaped bruises left afterward on their arms. With these points of reference, he was able to reconstruct the story to his satisfaction. In a way, it was like reconstructing old fragmented poems, or like translating from one language to another, from a world of hard but sparse facts to a storyscape of soft, fulfilling fictions.

Orion sat down and was twitching lazily. The white splash of star across its chest was facing Timothy, and the cat's tail licked slowly from side to side across the grooved mouth of the tire. Timothy's hand closed around the gun and he lifted it in a shaky motion toward the window. His other hand closed around his wrist and might have felt for his pulse. He steadied his own hand as he raised the pellet gun to the hole in the map. He let out his breath slowly. Orion was looking directly at him now, as if it could see something preordained in the backside of the colored papers covering the windows and the black barrel protruding quietly from the paper and shattered glass.

Timothy watched through the sight of the gun as he shot Orion, and the cat collapsed like the barn, lazily in a heap. Timothy saw the cat break like car glass, into discrete, square, connected pieces, there for him to piece together when he needed to. He inhaled quickly and thought of showing his father the constellations he had made with the stolen maps and the constellations he had made in the sky. He could imagine his excitement with his dad watching, sitting under streaking fireworks, falling and exploding on the Fourth of July. He may have exhaled, but he did not walk away.

4 /

Overhead, the stars began to slowly wink out.

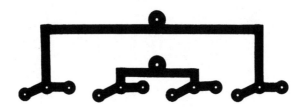

———— *Dear, distance is a long song   an equation   an incarceration*

I Am Getting
Comfortable With
My Grief

It fits in me like a fuse in a socket. Like a Swiss Army blade to a newfound cut. Like chalk or winter-pressure-crack to sidewalk. A scar on an arm. A shell in the belly. Popcorn shrapnel caught in your gum. We are not hard as if made of teeth. Our enamel soft and white like cream like butter like British food like the color rot-gray like most foods without artificial coloring like animals born and moving underground like used-up gum like light. The sky turns different colors with you gone: brack and murk. Liz, vines grow twice as fast in the week after your wake. The snow melts and shoots come up through it in the thinnest patches. This is not a sign of life continuing on, unabated. It is not symbolic of the new beginning I deserve so richly. Fir trees cease to be able to be burnt. They don't crack and spark hot in the fire. Fires die down. Even the birds keep low to the ground. Out of fear or out of respect, the sheerness of the face, the cliff stretching up a hundred feet above, we don our crampons and test the rope again. What can I say to mitigate the part I played in your disappearance in your death. What possible motive can I ascribe to its recording, to the economic problem it presents me with. Either write or wait. Either stew or spew. Either guilt or gild. I gild your story with grief with golf across a gulf with gold. It is the reorganization of a drawer. It is the skipping of stones across the asphalt on the highway. I cannot enter grief any more easily than my stones can penetrate the road. They can smash a windshield, though. They can maim a dog. They can rain pestilence on a bully. They can leave marks long tunnels like mines where they move into the snow. If I heat them in the fire and throw them with my gloves, they can evaporate the solid directly into gas.

The Sudden
Possibility of Nakedness

W hereas Liz is gone, I know, and there is only a slight emptiness now, a year after the fact, I still think she is somehow here—caught in the detritus dust attached to the pale green living room curtains, somewhere in the radio waves coming through the air, or perhaps misaddressed in the mail, eventually to find her way back to me. I don't know if this is a healthy feeling.

The town still feels lived in. The first slight spring thaw has begun, and the creek has started to run a bit more obviously underneath the ice. Sometimes I see a fish move there—a shadow hand—through the glassy surface, when I go down to the bed.

Jelly is getting married tonight—very early in the year because it's cheaper to do so, and he's always been one for bucking convention. Screw May or June he said. His wife-to-be—who is from out of state and whom I have not yet met—is all for it, since her family has never been to this part of the country. They call it a safari and they will bring their cameras. They are easily amused. They are tourists.

All of us who remain in Michigan or within a ten-hour drive have received these lovely invitations—hand-printed, it looks like, from a woodcut, of some flower that I can't identify because of poor artistry—and those who are willing to commit under threat of weather will be there. Those who want to celebrate another year gone by will be there. Some of us who are gone will make it up, and some of us will not.

There are some jet streaks across the sky, which is clear though not much warmer.

This bodes well I think. Some evidence of travel. Some evidence of departure and return.

My psychologist feels that 1) I need to talk more about my mother in order to clarify and then get over it, and 2) that I should go to the wedding—that seeing a relationship successful will do me good. He calls it modeling. I don't know if I should get over it at all. Should I pass it like a painful kidney stone? What is the proper metaphor for this? He says I am retreating into literature.

I say then what is literature for.

He becomes annoyed. He is not so good at what he does.

What I don't tell him is that I still think she's there—not just my mother, whom I think I sometimes hear but Liz my X whom I don't speak about with him. I don't tell him quite a bit. I'd rather keep it like a secret. But I will go to the wedding—taking place not in church but out at the breakers, the opening-out of the Portage canal into Lake Superior. I will go to the reception and enjoy myself.

The reception is by every definition swinging, as far as that goes up here. It takes place in a bar and restaurant on the seventh floor of the biggest motel in the area, and the place is packed. Mostly it is people I don't know too well, family of the bride and groom, but I recognize Sal Luoma, the Chemistry teacher from the old school, before the building went down in dynamite and dust, and the Vice Principal whom I only know through disciplinary action and repeated reprimand. I try to be jolly and say hello to both. Sal is genial if uptight, but I am glad to see her. Her class was one of my favorites in high school, I tell her, and a smile breaks across her face—another minor pleasure. I don't tell her that I salvaged what equipment I could from the Chemistry lab in the days before the school's demolition—Bunsen burners, long-necked pipettes, old beakers and flasks: items of serious classroom investigation, items that could be used for other purposes (fires, drugs, late night mad scientist action). I wonder what it must be like to teach school up here, but I don't tell her this.

Christer sits down next to me and tells me to check out the debacle. I'm sort of shocked to say that there is some *Macarena* going on. Bottles of vodka adorn every table like busts or ice hanging from the gutters of a roof. Some folks are getting hammered, but I'm trying to stay mostly dry; I feel like I owe it to someone, though I'm not sure yet who.

Christer and I have a sort of toast—to getting out, whatever the cost. To cost itself. To another year against the prospect of extinction. He is going downstate on scholarship for school (though I suspect it's seminary) next year, and though I have no plans, I am also leaving, though I am not sure yet where to or how.

Many of my parents' old friends are here. I've never seen them drunk and it's both loud and grand. I feel that I have been accidentally invited to a secret gathering—some sacrifice to the weather, for the return of warm air days—that this is not for me.

Christer is gone back to the dance floor on the invitation from a former classmate.

There is a disco ball throwing lights on all the walls and ceiling like fast-moving stars.

After the dancing has subsided for a time, there is some toasting. My psychologist, I realize to my horror, is completely schnitzeled. He is up on the table and rocking back and forth. He holds a bottle in one hand. Singing Tom Jones. Swinging his hips like Elvis. I fear the possibility of stripping.

I get out.

But first, using one of the disposable cameras set on every table—I'm sure ostensibly to be returned to the bride and groom—I take a couple shots for the sake of evidence. Just in case he confronts me later about my lack of action. This will exempt me from future dissection in his chair. I put it in my pocket, get my coat to go.

I make some plans to see those here who mean the most to me before they go back to their lives elsewhere, and I am out the door. I have done the best I could, I tell myself.

Darker outside than I had imagined—I must have stayed longer than I thought, and the curtain must have fallen. Slight evidence of *aurora borealis* beginning in the sky. There's plenty of snow bunched up around the sides of roads—just a rind of salt now along the edge of a glass—but nothing's coming down. It may actually be spring. I have filled out some postcards and put them in the mail, bound for Florida, Georgia, Harriet, and other far-off places.

Outside of the reception, I'm calmer. I am alone and quiet. I have some photos from the reception, and I augment those with several of the *Ranger III* down at the dock, moored for the season which is soon to end. I want to set it loose, adrift—let it coast down the canal out into the lake. Let it founder there.

I wonder where my brother is—I know at home, but doing what? Sitting by the woodstove? My father will be in the attic with his radio, I know. I've got my own equipment now and my own call sign, having passed the necessary tests, though I don't use it much. It's the best way to talk to him, since he's nearly always on the airwaves someplace. My mother is gone and out in ether, too. And Liz my only X, my once-and-then-it's-gone, she's gone (and even the thought of her is nearly gone). And yes the stories have subsided from the papers, in favor of the awfulness with Carrie, and Crisco's plans for revenge if they ever let out the guy who did it, if they let him get away. I have archived all of these, clipped them neatly out, kept them in a binder. I will use them like a record, a permanent receipt.

The *Ranger III* is dark of course. There is only the one light illuminating the top to make sure that nobody accidentally rams it with a low-flying turboprop. There are the lights on top of the lift bridge that strobe quickly on and off, probably for the same reason. We adorn the things we love as charms against destruction. They remind me of the reception that I just left and all that healthy modeling.

I think about egging it but don't.

The air—though I keep telling myself it must be springy—is still definite and cold. I hear no snowmobiles revving through town, or gunning their engines across the frozen canal. Even they must know it's too risky now.

There is a metal scent. The Burger King is filled with the usual set of goons.

A plow ambles uselessly along the street.

There are lights along both sides of the canal, like an airstrip. It's dark enough that they also look like stars. They make a sort of constellation, but of what I don't much know. An ambulance shriek goes by—doppler—on the way to the hospital. They sound different from every side—the horn from each side makes a different sound, so that you know from which way the thing is coming, and you know to pull your car over and get out of the way. I know this because I read about it, and asked one of the EMT guys when I was at the hospital a month ago with my brother who was having difficulty breathing.

I see a black cat dash from an alleyway into a dumpster. It must be warming up.

Everything, I think, is full of stars. The road, the sky, the glass storefronts of businesses downtown.

There is a possibility of recovery, I think. Look at Pastor Sam, who had a stroke—was nearly dead to the world, an unlit buoy, and who recovered from it most of the way, enough to continue his (still dull) sermons on Sundays. That is a start, a fresh toilet paper roll, a bulb placed in new soil after winter—expense and expectation.

So I walk home. I have my undeveloped photographs. One of the boarded-up opening into the mine, a couple of the *Ranger*. Several of the reception and its hilarity or lack thereof. One or two in which I hope that Liz will appear, a ghost moving like static electricity through the crowd. I can feel her in the warming air. More accurately, I feel something in the warming air, but I'm not sure it's her. Of course it's not her, but there is something—a familiar scent or haze, a far-off tone. The space that fire or light has left. Remainders on the retina. I have spent so much time on Liz, I wonder if it's her I loved or the loss itself.

At home I have my Bunsen burners, some broken concrete blocks, and several other salvage items from the wreckage of the school. The rice packet from the after-wedding, which I didn't tear open to throw (there was enough of it to go around, I thought). Little souvenirs from a long year.

The site of the old school is where I end up. Fences ring the thing to keep people out. Crash scene with police tape and flashing light. Concentration camp.

I had thought I'd be ecstatic to see it fall, the demise of school, you know, that Alice Cooper dream—even skipped work the day they brought it down to watch the demolition—but I was not. It just left me with an ache. What a huge building. What engineering and meticulous construction. What asbestos was used in there, too pricey to remove. What stories contained there, down by the boiler room, in the gym that doubled as a lunchroom and as a result reeked something awful, what stories in the classrooms devoted to Chemistry and Health.

When it came down I felt somehow left behind, as if I should have been in it when it went (and don't think I didn't consider it, sneaking in during the night, suicide by massive demolition and collapse), or should have somehow sent it off.

Now it is just a wreck, like the wrecks of ships littering the floor of Lake Superior, like the wrecks of snowmobiles and cars in the canal and in the lake. It is like a lot of things, I think. It will be sold and built up again as something else. An office complex. An old folks home. A new Country & Western radio station.

The moon is out, illuminating another recent jet trail that is breaking apart even as it is revealed. Back into gas, humidity, and velocity.

I am suddenly warm. Begin to take off my clothes in layers.

I have much to do.

I will go back to Tapiola to see what's in store for me.

I will go back to the radio and its long distance dedications.

I will go back to reading all my mail, from Canada or not.

I will go back to my phones that branch out of this place.

I will bring my brother back to Paulding, and we will sit on the hood of the still-warm car and breathe our dragon breath into the air and watch that weird light come slowly closer.

Dear, everything has a source
if you can find it, some
point of emanation ———————

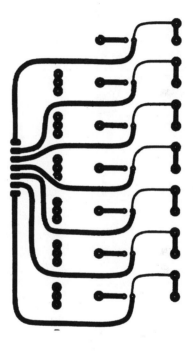

An Index to the Text

AND A RECORD AND CONCORDANCE OF OBSESSIONS

absence, 44, 86, 99; of arm, 33; of
  Bernard, 84–6; of Carrie, 150;
  of Liz, 32, 36, 63, 64, 65–8,
  69–71, 145–6, 151–2; of
  mothers, 33, 39, 104, 114,
  121–3, 150; of snow, 73; of
  stars, 143; in toilet stall, 35; of
  uncles, 21; of visions, 86
accident, 10, 19, 32, 97, 104, 152;
  auto, 30, 33, 36, 47, 60, 63, 64,
  66, 68, 95; shop-class, 32–4;
  snowmobile, 27, 30, 33, 35,
  37–8, 66, 80–1, 102, 152
Aerostar, 46, 51, 73, 79
Amis, Martin, 105–111
an anecdote, reconstructed: after
  prom with Liz—after prom
  with Liz with streamers in
  their pockets. Streamers torn
  down from the new school
  gym, mementos of the dance.
  Liz and Jesse as friends, not
  dates. On their way out to Gay,
  Michigan, where the after-
  party was. Saw something in
  the road. Not drinking,
  talking. Listening to Cowboy
  Junkies. Some light in the car
  from those they passed. Still
  ice on the ground of course up
  here in Spring. More light

leaking out from the
fluorescence on his watch as
he checks it because his
Toyota's clock does not work.
He slides the sunroof open so
Liz can see the moon, so she
can be happy. Cigarette light in
passing cars. Dashboard's low
emissions. Starlight: very old.
An occasional streetlamp or
jack-o-lantern out of season
on a porch. Candles lit inside.
A premonition of fire,
upcoming accident, 3, 25, 27,
61, 64–5, 68
architecture, 31, 49
arms & armlessness, 11, 15, 17, 27,
  33, 46, 48, 66, 83, 85, 87, 91,
  92, 93, 98, 108, 113, 129–31,
  133, 134, 142, 145
axe, 3, 31, 32

barn, collapsed, 49, 95, 104, 135,
  138
beacon, warning, 42, 59, 106
Bernard, 30, 83–94
blizzards, 8, 21–3, 95–7, 103–4,
  105; *see also* snow
blood: as emblem of ancestry, 21;
  as emblem of necessity, 22, 46,
  114, 126; as emblem of

Appendix

NOTES ON SOURCES AND FURTHER THANKS

Thanks to:

Sandy Huss, especially, who oversaw the taming of the beast (inasmuch as it was tamed).

Michael Martone, Steve Miller, Wendy Rawlings, and Bruce Smith, who were all in on its initial incarnation.

Deb Marquart, Robin Metz, Audrey Petty, and Sheryl St. Germain, for their patience and belief.

Sarah Gorham, Nickole Brown, and others at Sarabande, for taking a chance on this strange thing; and certainly Kirby Gann, who helped refine this immeasurably.

Much of this book was originally part of a collaboration, *Slow Dancing Through Ether*, with book artist Kris Ingmundson. A note about the project [which can be seen in more detail at <otherelectricities.com/oe>]: *Slow Dancing Through Ether* is a series of five unique books that attempts an integration of content and structure. Each book incorporates text and artwork, and is handbound in pink Nigerian goatskin. The leather that covers the text is featured as skin, with the wounds and imperfections of the body—the bindings are a sort of amputation. The reader holding these innovative structures experiences a lack of control and a sense of discomfort that is a reflection of the text. I did the interiors (taken from this manuscript) of three of the books. Kris did the interiors of the remaining two as interpretations of my work. The wonderful bindings are all hers. Hence big thanks to Kris. These books must be seen (or, better, held) to be believed. Take a look at the Web site for photographs and more detail.

Alicia Holmes, for her good eyes and ears as this manuscript unfolded.

A few others who have helped in their own ways with the book's construction: Megan Campbell, Lauren Goodwin, Sophia Kartsonis, Christopher Roman, Emma Ramey, Andy Segedi, Ali Stine, and Matt Vadnais. I'm probably forgetting people here; I hope that they'll forgive this omission.

Rob Y. and Matt F., Jeremiah M., Lisa P., plus many more whose parts may all appear in parts. If they are here at all, they are barely here, and poorly represented. And absolutely the Watts family. Same goes to the rest of my own family and friends for their roles in this.

"To Reduce Your Likelihood of Murder" won the 2004 World's Best Short-Short Contest and appeared in *The Southeast Review.* Thanks to Julia Glass for seeing something there.

"Other Electricities" won the 2002 *Fugue* magazine fiction prize. Thanks to Rick Moody for being entertained.

Alan Sparhawk, Zak Sally, and Mimi Parker from the Duluth (Minnesota) band Low, for providing a kind of soundtrack to this book (certainly to the writing of the book). See especially the albums *Trust, Secret Name, Long Division,* and *I Could Live in Hope.* For more information, go to <chairkickers.com>. I will refund your money if you don't like their music.

The last line from "Constellations" is pretty closely cribbed from a Ray Bradbury story.

"Forecast" takes after Martin Amis's *London Fields* in its own way.

"The Sudden Possibility of Nakedness" includes a line taken, sort of, from a Sundays song.

Radio schematics provided courtesy of *The ARRL Handbook,* 1985
edition. Used by permission.

Megan Campbell

The Author

Ander Monson grew up in the Upper Peninsula of Michigan. He lived briefly in Saudi Arabia, Iowa, and in the Deep South, where he received his MFA from the University of Alabama. He is the editor of the magazine *DIAGRAM* <http://thediagram.com> and the New Michigan Press. His stories, essays, and poems have appeared in many literary magazines, including *The North American Review, Fence, FIELD, Gulf Coast, The Bellingham Review, Ploughshares, Boston Review,* and *Mississippi Review.* He teaches at Grand Valley State University and lives in Grand Rapids, Michigan, with his wife, Megan, and three cats. Tupelo Press recently published his poetry collection, *Vacationland.*